PLEASE DON'T GO, GIRL

LOVE ONE THE RADIO
BOOK 3

NAIMA SIMONE

$$1$$

_____

Lena

I'm a jealous bitch.

God, I wince as I even think that. It's terrible—both calling myself a bitch and, worse, being jealous. I'm not that person. Or...at least I thought I wasn't. But as I look at my best friend, Lennon Ward, with King Sullivan, lead singer of Bloody Sunday, one of the most famous and iconic rock bands of our time, I own my shit.

Lifting my glass to my mouth, I swallow the cranberry and vodka along with a sigh.

It's so not becoming to envy my girl. Especially knowing everything she and King went through to get to this place. And I don't mean in the VIP section of a Seattle club. They've been through a decade long separation, secrets, addiction, loved ones in opposition of their relationship... My girl deserves all the happiness and this amazing future with the first and only man she's loved. They both do.

Which makes this dirty, oily thing slinking through my veins even more profane.

Damn.

I need more alcohol.

Standing from the leather couch, I keep my gaze focused on the empty glass and not on the black matching leather armchair where Lennon is perched on King's lap, the both of them oblivious to the partying going on around them.

I approach the bar on the far end of the VIP suite, order another cranberry and vodka—my third, but who's counting?—and after receiving it, head over to the smoked window that offers a view of the lower level of the club. It's packed with people dancing on the huge dance floor in front of the elevated DJ's booth, sitting at the scattered high tables or bellied up to the two bars that line either side of the club. The spacious VIP rooms sit high above the floor, like royals separating themselves from the masses.

Under ordinary circumstances, I would never have been granted access to this rarified space. But these circumstances aren't ordinary, by any means. I mean, just six months ago, my idea of excitement was half off margaritas at The Hammerhead, the local bar—well, only bar—in Pike's End, my hometown. Now, I'm attending sold out concerts for one of the world's most popular bands and partying with them in a club. Life is truly unpredictable and funny. Not funny, *ha ha* either. Just plain...weird.

Sighing, I blindly stare out the wall of glass and try to analyze the source of this knot of heaviness in my chest. Here I am, surrounded by rock royalty, a foot in a world I could only fantasize about, and I'm...blah.

"Hey, best friend." An arm slides around my waist, and a moment later, a body a little shorter than my five feet, six inch frame presses against my side. "Given the amount of alcohol freely flowing around here, you look awfully down."

Smiling, I wrap my arm around her shoulders and squeeze.

"One, I've been taking full advantage of the cornucopia of booze." I hold up my newly refilled glass of cranberry and vodka as Exhibit A. "And I just have to say, rock stars come with the top shelf shit. Which is good given my exceptional and picky palate." We stare at each other then, a second later, snicker. Picky palate, my ass. I've been known to snatch up the remnants of a Long Island Iced Tea and mix it with a rum and Coke on a girls' night simply because I don't believe in alcohol going to waste. Why, yes, I'm classy like that. "And two, how can you possibly know what I look like when you've been over there playing *The Good Doctor* with King?"

Lennon tips her head back on a loud crack of laughter. I grin, adoring this happiness on her. She's wearing it as well as the black leather pants wrapped around her gorgeous legs and ass.

What? I can admire.

"Look, Dr. Shaun Murphy is the shit, not to mention very thorough and dedicated to his work. So I'm taking that as a compliment." Lennon bumps my hip with hers. "But don't try and dodge the subject. I know when there's something wrong with you. That's what happens when you've been best friends since the fifth grade. Now, spill it. What's going on with you?"

I lift my drink for a long sip, avoiding immediately answering. Lennon's not wrong; we've been in each other's lives since Mrs. Gilbert's class, and I got moved to the front because I couldn't stop running my mouth. Lennon's desk had been next to mine, and it's been history from there.

But confessing to her that I'm an ugly shade of green over the love, safety and stability she's found? I can't bring myself to do it. That's making my feelings, my—my burden hers, and that's not fair. Especially since there's nothing she can do about it. Hell, I don't even know how to address it or how...ugly it makes me feel.

"Truthfully?" I mentally wince. "It's a little surreal. And I'm still trying to convince myself that I'm actually here and this isn't some fever dream brought on by too much allergy medicine."

Not a lie. Exactly.

I turn slightly and covertly scan the VIP room, trying not to appear like I'm gawking. But let's be clear —I'm indeed gawking.

A crowd of the most gorgeous people I've ever seen are packed into the glassed in room, talking, laughing, drinking. They're sprawled on the three leather couches and chairs, sitting on the table, pressed to the floor-to-ceiling windows. And among them are King Sullivan, Gideon Dunn, Mac Bowman and Kade Gibson, the members of Bloody Sunday.

Against my will, my gaze lingers on Kade Gibson. The drummer is known for his raw ferocity and creative, unique fills and amazing intros, as well as his versatility—it's common knowledge he can play three different instruments and has several songwriting credits, including some of their biggest hits. He's basically a legend in the music world.

But all that talent and genius isn't why I'm staring.

That man is a walking pheromone.

Big, blond and bearded, he could be a throwback to a time of longships, raids and pagan gods. Hell, he'd even taken to wearing braids in the beard he'd grown out and three or four cornrows in the long, thick hair with its shaved sides. On any other person, it would look pretentious and like a gimmick. But on him, with his broad shoulders, wide chest and thick thighs, and those gorgeous arms that should have their own porn site, he's just...perfect.

As if he senses my gaze on him, he lifts his head, looking away from the two women cuddled up against his large frame and fixes those light green eyes on me. A shiver races down my spine, crackling and snapping like fireworks. Thank God he can't see my reaction to him. I mean, surely the man is used to women throwing themselves at his feet. But for some insane reason, I don't want to be one of the herd to him. Which in itself is nuts. Though I'm a friend of his best friend's fiancée, he hasn't said more than two things to me. "Hi" and "what's up."

Oh no. I lied. There was the time he said, "Get off my foot" when I was indeed standing on his foot at King and Lennon's engagement party a couple of months ago. So seven words. He hasn't said more than seven words to me. So I'm not one of *anything* to the drummer. I might as well be the wall.

Which I'm good with, especially considering my last relationship went up in smoke—like literally. I threw a bag of flaming dog shit on his porch. Allegedly.

But that shit show—no pun intended—was with a regular-degular officer-at-a-bank guy. What the hell would I do with a rock star? I'd probably end up committing a felony instead of a misdemeanor. Again...allegedly.

Not that I would ever be in a relationship with Kade Gibson. Nothing in that beautifully sculpted face of stark angles and lush curves screams *commitment*. Nope. Instead it yells, *Sit on my face, nut, and then get out.*

Just as images of what the drummer's mouth could

probably do with my thighs caging his face, Kade arches a dark blond brow. *Holy shit.* I jerk my head back around, humiliation scorching a path straight to my face and sorely abused soul. What am I? A damn magnet for embarrassment? Other people attract good vibes and karma. I'm the opposite. Assholes and mortification are more my jam.

"Hey, you okay?" Lennon tilts her head, frowning at me, and the concern in her eyes is hard to miss. Even with my itchy contacts.

I shake my head and squeeze her shoulders before dropping my arm.

"I'm perfectly fine. Stop worrying about me. You should be celebrating your man having an amazing show, nothing else."

A smile erases her frown, and the love that brightens her eyes as she glances over her shoulder toward King has that uncomfortable pinch in my chest reappearing with a vengeance. I'm the worst friend. And the shame wading in my belly like an Olympic swimmer has me looking away from her and back out the wall of glass.

"They were wonderful, weren't they?" she murmurs. "I'm so thrilled for King. For all of them. King has worked so hard on his sobriety, and he's been worried that his addiction, rehab and assuming care of Gunner might affect the band, the reception from their fans as well as the patience of the label. But I think tonight proved they're as great, if not better than before."

I nod. "Absolutely. They blew any doubts out of the water tonight."

For a time, King Sullivan had become the rock star cliché—a slave to sex, drugs and rock 'n' roll. Bloody Sunday's lead singer had fallen down that dark, ugly rabbit hole of addiction, and only after almost losing his life and his band did he finally enter rehab. And only days after leaving, he discovered he had a son and became a single dad. Then he returned to his hometown and reunited with his first love. It has been an eventful year, and yes, articles had popped up as well as posts on social media questioning if Bloody Sunday would recover from blow after blow, mainly inflicted by their mercurial lead singer.

But the last few months had proven that they were back with a vengeance. And I'm so thrilled for them and for my girl.

"Selling out Climate Pledge Arena out?" I shake my head. "All the haters can suck it."

Lennon laughs. "Hell, yeah, they can. And I'm going to let you get away with lying to me—for now. We've been friends for years, and if you think I can't tell when there's something bothering you, then you've probably had too much of that free liquor."

I snort, and this time, don't bother contradicting her. Like she said, we've been friends for a long time—since the fifth grade to be exact—and I should've known better than to lie to her.

"Fine. But not tonight." I lean forward and give her cheek a loud, smacking kiss. "Tonight is about that man of yours and that band of his, and you."

"I love you, woman."

I roll my eyes. "Duh, of course you do. What's not to love?"

Smirking, Lennon looses my waist and grabs my hand, tugging me toward the VIP door.

"Let's go."

I groan and cast a longing look down at my empty glass then over my shoulder toward the bar. "Where? Why must we leave all the booze?"

"Girl, it'll be here when we get back." Lennon laughs, continuing to drag me out the door. I pass the burly, bald security guard with shoulders that stretch the limits of his black suit jacket and hand him my glass. His expression doesn't change as he accepts it, but I mouth a, *Sorry*, to him anyway. "We're going to shake our asses on that dance floor," Lennon throws over her shoulder as she descends the stairs. "By the time you sweat the alcohol out of your pores, you'll be ready to drink some more."

"You should've led with we're making room for more vodka," I mutter.

She shakes her head, chuckling. A moment later, when she pulls open the door at the bottom of the steps, the deafening music and noise that the lofty— and soundproof—VIP section had muted slams into me like a tidal wave of sound. For a moment, it's a bit disorienting, and I draw to a halt, feeling the heavy bass throb inside of me.

I briefly close my eyes and inhale the scent of smoke, sweat and beer, trapping it in my lungs. It's been forever since I've been out in this kind of setting. And The Hammerhead, Pike's Peak's only bar, doesn't count since there's no other place to go. In the past few months I haven't felt like...partying. And I hate that for myself. I used to be the one dragging Lennon to the bar for the live band performances or coercing her into accompanying me to the nightclubs in nearby cities. I would be that person who decided on Monday to visit New York City and fly out there days later. That spontaneous, life-embracing woman who laughed loud and long, who anticipated and enjoyed every day with the surprises it would bring has been missing in action. Maybe I should put her face on a milk carton and see if I can track her down. Because who I've become—this wary, overly cautious, emotionally defeated woman—has overstayed her welcome.

And I'm tired of her.

Tired of myself.

"Hey." Lennon squeezes my hand. "You good?" she asked for the second time in minutes.

"Yes." I smile, returning what I hope is a reassuring smile. "Now, let's go before my back and hips remember that I'm too fucking old to be twerking."

Laughing, she said, "Bet."

With a wide grin, I follow behind her, suddenly eager to get to that dance floor and just let loose. I need the release, the freedom.

"Damn, it's thick as hell in—oh, sorry!" The apology spills from my lips when I slam into someone's back. My palms fly up, bracing myself against their back. At my touch, the person whips around. "My ba—Ben?"

My voice drops to a barely there whisper as my ex-boyfriend scowls down at me, his dark blue eyes narrowing as recognition and surprise flares in them. My heart swan dives toward my stomach, and my lips part, but no sound emerges. Everything in me freezes, and a sleet of ice skates over my skin. His mouth turns down at the corners, and they move but I can't hear anything —not him, not the music—over the throbbing sound of my pulse in my ears.

This isn't happening.

This isn't *fucking happening.*

It's not possible that I'm hours away from home and I run into my asshole of an ex-boyfriend.

All of the tension I'd just released rushes back in like a flood, dousing me in the insecurity, hurt and anger I've hoarded like a jealous dragon. It's been months since Ben dumped me, and yet the powerlessness and confusion still linger and clings to me like mold.

A hand squeezes mine, and I glance down at Lennon's fingers still clasped tightly around mine as if it's my first time noticing it. Lifting my gaze to hers, I focus on the fierce frown darkening her beautiful face, and I study it, desperately clinging to it. In this moment, it's my lifeline, the only thing saving me from drowning in the toxic emotions threatening to tug me under.

Lennon jerks her chin up, silently asking me if I was okay. I force my head to dip in in a nod, and she jerks around to face Ben, not bothering to disguise her disgust with him.

"Lena?" His gaze scans over me, and his lip curves at the corner as if my gold, off-the-shoulder bandage dress and stiletto heels are obscene and personally offends his sensibilities. Sadly, this expression is nothing new to me—the expression or the derision. "What're you doing here?" he sneers.

"Don't talk to her." Lennon steps forward, partially blocking his view of me. "Better yet, if you have anything to say why not write it in a letter. I've heard you're really good at that," she snaps, referring to the Dear John letter he left on my dining room table, informing me that he was through with me and our relationship.

Fucking coward.

Ben's glare shifts from Lennon to me, his anger like a physical touch, and I shudder at the touch of it. Hating it. Part of me can't believe I ever let this mu'-fucka put his hands on me, much less allow him inside my body.

But then there's the other part that peruses my boyfriend choices in the past, and well, yeah. That part of me totally accepts that I added Ben to my toxic list. It's like if there's an asshole, cheap douche or condescending prick within a five mile radius, I go hunt him down and jump on his cock with destructive and reckless abandon.

I'm truly my father's daughter.

Only he was indiscriminate about pussy, not dick.

Speaking of dicks...

"I see you're still running to your little friend with our business," Ben says to me, ignoring Lennon. "Nothing's changed, I see."

I stiffen and my own eyes narrow as anger surges inside me, incinerating the other emotions to ash. Hold the fuck up. Denigrating me is one thing. But my girl? Fuck that.

"Little friend?" I snort and roll my eyes. "Yeah, nothing's changed, Ben. You're still the pretentious, patronizing asshole you've always been."

His nostrils flare, and his lips tighten into a flat, forbidding line. But before he can come back at me—and this is Ben, he will definitely snap back—a pretty woman slides in closer to him, pressing her impressive breasts to his arm.

"Babe," she practically coos, her long, dark, bone straight hair, falling over her slim shoulder as she tips her head back and gazes up at him through impossibly long lashes. "Are you going to introduce me?"

A pang of hurt stabs me in the chest, and goddamn, I want to tear my heart out and fling it across the club. It's a foolish thing that has brought me nothing but pain, and it can't fucking read. A. Room.

This man has discarded and disrespected me. I shouldn't give a fuck if he's with Pennywise the Clown much less another woman. But...I do. I care. Because once again, it proves how expendable and unloved I was—I am.

Tears prick my eyes, and it shouldn't have been possible to loathe myself more in this moment, but apparently, I'm plumbing new depths.

"Danielle, this is Lena." He pauses, and though he's talking to her, his voice easily carries to me. Because it's meant for me to hear. "She's the one I was telling you about."

A fist of pure humiliation slams into my chest, and when a smile comprised of both pity and disgust curves Corrine's mouth, I can barely expel air from my lungs. I knew Ben was a douche, but what did I ever do to him to deserve his...cruelty? Right now, I begrudge my vivid imagination because it immediately provides crystal clear images of just what he's said about me, how he's portrayed me as some unstable, obsessed ex.

Fuck him.

No, *fuck. Him.*

Speak, dammit. Rip him a new hole to shit out of. Do something other than stand here, mute with tears burning your eyes.

I try to obey that vicious voice in my head that's demanding Ben's figurative blood, but I can't move. Can't speak. And when I part my lips, it's only to drag in a trembling breath.

"The hell you mean the one you told her about?" Lennon snarls, fury quivering in her voice. She takes a step toward Ben and his new girlfriend. "You know what? You can fu—"

"What's up, baby? You left the VIP area without me." The question rumbles in my ear only seconds before a muscled pair of tattooed arms close around me and a hard chest presses to my back.

I should know that chest and those arms—I've stared at them enough over the years and up close and personal in the last few months. But no, it's the gravel roughened, low voice that sounds as if it's traveled over miles and miles of pitted road that clues me in to wrap me in a strong, strangely comforting embrace.

Without my permission, my muscles loosen, and I sink against Kade Gibson, allowing his big body to brace me. But then...*hold the fuck up.*

Baby?

He called me "baby."

I frown, shock rippling through me in dissonant waves. Bloody Sunday's drummer who I haven't even held a full conversation with suddenly holding me and calling me by an endearment? Nope. The math ain't mathing.

"What is—*mmph.*"

Oh my God.

Kade Gibson is kissing me.

That beautiful, carnal mouth that I'm slightly ob-sessed with possessed mine like he owned the title to it. And holy hell, I would sign everything over to him.

The shock ricocheting through me ebbed, and pure pleasure blazed a path through me. I locked down the moan that rappelled up my throat and tried to break free. I can't lie and say I hadn't imagined this man's mouth on me. What it would feel like to have his cover mine, shape it to fit his. And now, as his tongue laps at my lips before slipping between and sweeping inside with a possessive stroke, demanding I meet him, engage with him, I can say with crystal clarity that imagination doesn't compare to reality. It's sooo much better.

That groan escapes me, and a big, calloused hand curves around my jaw, holding me still for a deeper claiming. And I'm helpless under the sensual on-slaught... No, that's not correct. Helpless implies I have no choice, no power. And this kiss, this tender but greedy fucking of my mouth is the hill I'm willing to die on.

With one last lick, he lifts his head, and *damn*, I chase his mouth. All shame and modesty crumbled to dust in the pursuit of one last taste of him. Those bright green eyes gleam from under hooded lids, and he obliges me, pecking my lips one last time before lowering his hand.

"Don't you dare give this motherfucker your tears. He doesn't deserve them, and he sure as fuck doesn't get to see them," Kade growls, low enough that his admonishment, as blistering as the kiss he just delivered, only reaches my ears.

My breath catches in my throat, and I blink. Those beautiful, almost eerily bright eyes don't release me. For several long seconds, he holds me captive. Then with a small, almost imperceptible nod he glances away from me and focuses his gaze over my head.

On Ben.

The arm around my waist tightens, but his voice is casual...taunting.

"*Ah*." Kade draws the word out, nodding slowly. "You're the ex. It's making sense now."

Ben's face screws up as if he just tasted something foul. *God.* What did I ever see in this asshole?

"Oh my God! It's you!" Ben's girlfriend practically screams.

If she whipped out a marker and demanded he sign her very impressive cleavage, I wouldn't be shocked. At all.

Ben throws her a poisoned glare, but he could've

saved the effort. She doesn't notice his visual "What the hell?" because she's too busy eye-fucking Kade.

Now, Kade isn't my man, but damn, *she* doesn't know that.

Just rude.

"Yes, I'm her ex. Thank God for the *ex* part. And what makes sense?" Ben sneers.

Kade skims his lips over my temple. Back and forth. Back and forth in a hypnotic caress that has me leaning further into the big, solid shelter of his body. What is this magic...?

Kade's low chuckle vibrates against my back.

"Why she comes so fast and often on my cock. Deprivation isn't a pretty thing. Oh wait, I take that back." He lowers his head and brushes a hot kiss with a hint of tongue over my jaw, and holy hell, my mind blanks as I choke back a whimper. My horror and outrage at his bald, rude as fuck announcement of how I come—which he possesses no biblical knowledge of—are drowned out by the deluge of lust at that flick of his tongue over my skin. "Deprivation isn't pretty unless it's the sight of this greedy little pussy getting all wet," he continues on a growl.

The fuck? Did he just...? Hell no, he didn't... Did he?

Ben's gasp covers my own. Part of me wants to turn around and slap a hand over that diabolical mouth. The other part? Well that hussy is preening. Even though I know Kade's intentions, and I appreciate this whole charade, I should still be mortified at how he's going about it. And I am...sorta...kinda...

Okay, shit, I'm turned on and horrified. The two do not have to be mutually exclusive.

King's low chuckle cuts through the noise in my head—and the chaotic swirl of lust and need in my body—and for the first time, I notice him standing beside Lennon. That just goes to show the power of Kade's sexual magnetism. I'm blind to whole people now.

Kade's hand slides over my trembling belly and his spread fingers continue down, down...

"Kade," I grind out, circling his wrist and halting his trajectory.

There's zero remorse in that utterly debauched, rumbling laugh—or in the fingers that drum a soundless beat just above my mound. That rhythm echoes through my pussy, pulsing in my clit.

Oh God. What is he doing to me?

"Sorry, baby. TMI?" he asks, pinching my chin and tilting my head to the side and back so I have no choice but to meet his hooded green gaze. Humor gleams there, but so does a flinty, sharp glint that promises pain, hurt—and not mine.

"Yes, just a skosh," I grind out.

"My bad." He grins and it's completely unrepentant.

Switching his attention back to Ben, he jerks his chin up.

"Sorry," he says to my ex, but the wide smile kind of ruins the sentiment. "How 'bout I buy you and your girl a round of drinks as a show of apology?"

He circles his hand around the base of my throat, and though he doesn't squeeze, the weight of his palm against the front of my neck has need pumping through my veins like a drug.

"No," Ben snaps.

"Sure!" his girlfriend chirps.

Lennon snickers as I arch an eyebrow. Really, girl? Either she's not reading the room either and has no loyalty or she's really thirsty. From the way her gaze is glued to Kade with a lascivious gleam in her eye, I'm thinking it's option A.

From the tight, pinched set of his face, I'm guessing Ben thinks the same.

"I gotchu," Kade said, and the other's woman smiles so big I can count all thirty-two teeth in her mouth.

I try not to roll my eyes, but the struggle is real.

"I said I—" Ben growls, but Kade turns to one of the bodyguards behind him, cutting my ex off midsentence. Or mid complaint.

"Hey, Steve, can you send Damon up to VIP?" When the bodyguard nodded and pulled out his phone, Kade shifted his attention back to Ben and... yeah, I don't know her name. "Damon's the owner of this place. He'll hook you up, and it's on me."

"That's so generous of you," the brunette purrs. "Thank you so much."

Ben balls his face up, and leans down, whispering something in her ear. When she twists her mouth up and hisses something back, Kade chuckled, the sound low and mean in my ear.

It's petty—God knows it is. But am I enjoying this? Why yes, yes, I am.

"Think nothing of it." Kade waves a hand. "As a matter of fact, you should really thank Lena, I'm trying to get back in good with her." He shifts to my side, hooking his arm around my neck. "How'd I do, baby?" he asks, tilting my head up with a gentle nudge of his fingers. "Forgive me?"

"Sure," I drawl.

The corner of his mouth quirks, and my gaze dips to it. And lingers. My lips tingle with the memory of how he claimed mine just minutes ago. I curl my fingers into a fist, prohibiting them from ghosting over my mouth.

But a flare of heat flashes in his eyes, and they narrow. I'm not a mind reader, and I can't decipher his thoughts. If I was, though, I'm pretty sure he's thinking, *Yes, I fucked that mouth, and you took it like the good girl you are.*

Or maybe I'm projecting.

My thighs tremble as his teeth sink into his full bottom lip.

Definitely. I'm definitely projecting.

"You ready to head back up? I got plans for you," he says with a wicked grin.

Giving Ben and his girlfriend a chin jerk, he turns around, taking me with him. Not that I'm fighting his maneuvering. Hell if I want to stay here with Ben. Even the urge to dance has evaporated since I now know my ex is somewhere in this building.

"Just don't break up with her," Ben calls out, seeming to find his balls back after Kade walks off. "As crazy as she is, you'll end up with a stalker on your hands."

Kade snaps to a halt, drawing me to a stop as well. Not that I can move anyway. Guilt and shame winds through me like a grimy oil spill. I'm not proud of what I did, how I lost myself to pain, rage and humiliation. And Ben will never let me forget it.

Slowly, Kade unwraps his arm from around me and pivots on his heel, facing my ex again. One glance at the drummer's cold, impassive expression, and I reach for him. Pretending to be my man is one thing, but doing something foolish that he can't take back in the name of the ruse? No, I can't allow that. Especially when he has so much to lose. Ben is the kind of POS that will have him arrested then turn around and sue

Kade just so he can feel superior and put him "in his place."

After the last few years Bloody Sunday has had, he doesn't need any kind of trouble or bad press. Especially not over this.

Not over me.

"Kade," I murmur, caution.

My grip slides down his arm and for a moment, his huge, warm hand enfolds mine, squeezing. But other than that, he ignores my attempt to forestall him, gently shaking off my clasp.

"What did you say?" Kade softly asks, stalking closer to my ex.

And being the arrogant and totally oblivious asshole that he is, Ben doesn't notice when the current arrangement of his face is in dire trouble of being reassembled like a jigsaw puzzle.

"I said, she's cra—" Ben repeated, only to be cut off by a fist snatching the front of his shirt and twisting in the material so Kade's knuckles bumped up against the underside of Ben's chin.

With an embarrassing squeak, Ben rises to the tips of his toes, his fingers locking around Kade's wrist in a futile attempt to pry his hand off him.

"Here's the thing, Ben. Even if I was looking for relationship advice, it wouldn't be from your bitch ass. Because only a bitch takes jabs at a woman he once claimed to love in an attempt to bring her down to the trash ass level he's on. Especially when the woman he's currently with stands right beside him."

Kade abruptly releases him with a hard shove to Ben's chest. A sneer curls the drummer's perfect lips, and even that has my sex pounding, desperate to have that cruel smirk pressed against it. Moving over it. Again.

Get your head out of your panties, woman.

"You're lucky I don't believe in violence," Kade continues, the brutal edge that just sharpened his voice smoothing out into one that's almost conversational. The drummer holds up his big hands, wiggling those long, elegant fingers. Beautiful hands. I hate that I notice. Hate even more it's not the first time I have. "National treasures, y'know. But while I might not believe in violence," he shifts back into Ben's space, "it's my security's religion. Now you let me hear Lena's name in your mouth again—no, fuck that. If your lips are moving and it looks like they're *shaping* her name, I'm going to have them beat your ass down so hard my knuckles will feel it. Understand me, *Ben*?"

Anger twists Ben's face, but apparently there are a few brain cells left in his head because he tightly nods. His narrowed glare darts to me but Kade shifts, blocking his view.

"Nope. Talking includes looking. Don't even let your eyes roam in her direction by mistake. Now get the fuck up outta here."

Ben's eyebrows jack down, and his chest puffs out as he belatedly tries to show some balls. *Bruh, don't bother.* He glances to the side at his new woman, who still hasn't managed to stop staring at Kade or King. If she knows like I do, she better shift those eyes somewhere else. My best friend don't play about her man. They took too long to get to where they are now—ten years. Forget girl power and black girl magic. Lennon will drag her down by the roots over that man.

"Just because you're some *rock musician*," Ben sneers the words with as much disdain as others would say *serial killer*, "doesn't mean you own this club. I have as much right to be here as you do."

"Wanna bet?" Kade cocks his head, studying Ben

as if he's something I *allegedly* set fire to on a porch. Without glancing over his shoulder, he calls out to his bodyguard. "Steve?"

"Yeah, Kade."

"Call Damon back. Tell him never mind about those drinks. But I do have unwanted guests that need to be removed."

"On it."

All the sanctimonious fury wipes free from Ben's expression, and shock has him blinking at Kade. But in the next moment, he recovers and he sputters, "You can't... You're not..."

Kade smirks, arching an eyebrow. "Oh, but I can. And I fucking did."

"But what about me? I didn't do anything," his girl-friend objects, casting a look at Ben then turning back to Kade. She steps forward and away from Ben, a pout turning her mouth down at the corners. "It isn't fair. He can go, but I want to stay."

Wow. I glance at Lennon, and she mouths, *Really?*

And apparently, Ben is of the same mind because he scowls, barking, "Danielle! You can't be serious."

Danielle. So her name is Danielle. Good to know. It was bugging me.

She shrugs. "I came here to drink and party. I'm not ready to leave."

"That's some cold shit right there," Kade drawls, cocking his head. "But nah, sweetheart. I'm a firm be-liever in, if we came together, we leave together. You might want to check your company in the future." He hikes his chin up. "Hey, Damon. Here are the tres-passers. Thanks for handling this for me."

I glance behind Ben and Danielle, and a tall, deli-cious specimen of a man stands behind the couple. His suit conforms to his powerful figure and long, gorgeous dreads frame model-worthy cheekbones and a wide, sensual mouth. *This* is Damon, the club owner? No wonder this place is so popular. People must pile in here just to fix their gazes on him.

"Not a problem," Damon says in a low drawl that contains hints of the South. "I adore being at your beck and call."

Kade grins, not the least offended or intimidated by the pointed sarcasm. "'Preciate you. And it's always a pleasure to bask in your sunny disposition."

Damon's face doesn't change although his mouth could've given the barest of quirks. "Sir. Ma'am." He nods at Ben and Danielle. "If you'll follow me." It isn't posed as a question or request and the bouncers that move forward punctuate that.

"I can't believe this," Ben snaps. But he also storms off past Damon, Danielle on his heels.

With a mock salute, Damon turns and follows them, disappearing into the teeming crowd.

"That. Was. Amazing," Lennon crows, giving a little shimmy. "Kade, you are my hero."

"Standing right here, baby," King reminds her, humor lacing his tone.

"As if I could forget." She rises on tiptoes and smacks a kiss on his mouth, but King cuffs the back of her neck and holds her in place for a deeper kiss.

And that quick, they're lost in one another.

Sighing, I turn to Kade, who's wearing a wry smile.

"Well, I think that's my cue to leave." I shake my head, and as I meet his bright gaze, it suddenly hits me that, Kade Gibson not only kissed me but rode to my rescue like some dragon-slaying knight out of a fairy tale. Though, with his sexy smirk and faded T-shirt and jeans, he's more villain than hero. "Thank you for," I wave my hand in the direction Ben was standing moments earlier, "that. You didn't have to but..."

My battered pride is glad he did for whatever reason. And I still didn't know those reasons. We've never even had a full conversation, which made his decision to play Captain America even more confusing.

"Yeah, I did," he says, voice firm. His gaze drops over me, roaming and lingering on places that tighten, bud and grow soaking wet. When he meets my eyes again, I'm breathing puffs of smoke, and am convinced that instantaneous orgasms are a thing. "Your ex? He's a prick. And usually I'm not with the bullshit, but play silly games, get silly prizes. He was on something tonight, and I didn't like it. And you didn't deserve it."

"How do you know?" I blurt out. He cocks his head, and heat rushed up from my gut, making a bee-line for my face. Unlike the flames licking at me just moments ago, this had nothing to do with lust, and everything to do with embarrassment. "Never mind." I flick a hand and give a small chuckle, desperately trying to laugh my question off. "I'm just talking non-sense. Ben has that effect on people."

I attempt laughing again, but goddammit, it comes out thick and a bit strangled. Another wave of mortifi-cation sweeps through me, crashes over me, and my eyes burn with the telltale oncoming of tears. And I'm horrified.

This isn't me. I'm not weepy. I'm not so fucking emotional. Usually, shit like this just rolls right off my back. But maybe it's the combination of my earlier bout of envy, unexpectedly seeing Ben and facing his vitriol, and Kade's damn near vicious defense of me.

It's too much, and I don't have the emotional band-width to deal with it all.

"Shit," I mutter, blinking and dipping my chin.

"Thanks again, Kade. I'm just going to..." I trail off, turning toward the VIP entrance but a hand cupping the back of my neck drew me to an abrupt halt.

I gasp at the hot flash of pure electricity that sizzles from the spot he touches, down my spine, wrapping around my lower belly. It pulses, and I stiffen at the nearly overwhelming wave of need that crashes through me.

This is crazy. Sure, I haven't had sex in months—six to be exact—but even my vaginal deprivation can't excuse my body's damn near visceral reaction to a simple touch.

"C'mere." Kade doesn't give me room to argue—not that I can. His hand still cuffing my nape, he guides me past the VIP entrance and King and Lennon, who are still hugged up. Without breaking stride, he guides me down a shadowed hallway that leads away from the main part of the club. Moments later, he stops in front of a door, and with a glance behind us, notches his chin up. "Don't let anyone in, all right, Steve?"

"You got it."

How sad is it that once again, this man blinded me to my surroundings? Until now, I hadn't even noticed the bodyguard trailing us. I shake my head, a little disgusted with myself, and Kade glances down at me, eyebrow arched. I give my head another shake, and he seems to accept my non-explanation. But he doesn't remove that piercing, too intense gaze from me even as he twists the knob and pushes the door open.

The light flicks on, and I glimpse a rather sparse but surprisingly large office. A large desk and chairs claim the middle of the room and a dark brown leather couch occupies the far wall. That's it. Just spartan, with no personality and no clues as to who it belongs to. Actually, with the file cabinets and numerous boxes stacked on one side of the room, it's giving storeroom.

"Can we be in here?" I ask, moving forward, losing his grip on me.

My whole body laments that fact.

"Since this is my office, I'm going to say yes."

I whip around, feeling my eyes round in surprise.

"Say what now?" I scan the office again as if a picture of him will appear on the wall, verifying his claim. "Your...office? How...?"

"I'm a silent partner in the club. Damon is the face of it and runs most of the day to day operations. We grew up together, and he's been my best friend since the third grade. Damon has a track record of successful clubs all over the country. When he talked about opening one up here in Seattle, it was a no-brainer to throw in with him."

I stare at him. Blink. Stare some more.

"What?" He moves over to the desk and leans against it.

"That's probably the most you've ever spoken to me at one time." I huff out a dry chuckle. "Hell, I didn't even think you knew my name, for real. And you did...*that* back there. And now I'm in here with you. Alone. Why?"

"You're going to have to be more specific. Why did I bring you in here? Or why did I pretend to be your man?"

"Yes."

He smirks, and once more those light green eyes travel over me, leaving my skin tingling. The color reminds me of the mints my grandmother used to have out on her coffee table for "guests." No wonder every time our gazes connected, a sense of...calm, of familiarity swam beneath the ever present lust. They remind me of the place I always felt safest.

I duck my head, and cross the room to the sofa, sinking down on one end of it. Space. Space is good. Already his scent of top shelf whiskey, skin and bad decisions permeates the room. I thought inserting a whole room between us would diminish it, but it's infiltrated my nostrils, sits on my tongue. I taste it...taste him.

"First, let's clear something up," he says, rubbing his fingers through his thick beard. I fist my hand, but even my nails digging into my palm can't detract from the prickling across my skin. A prickling to feel that thick, coarse hair sliding through my own fingers. "I've always known your name. *Lena.*"

How he says my name should be illegal. How my nipples bead and my sex trembles at the sound of that low, raspy voice wrapping around my name should be punishable by firing squad.

"Let's start why I pretended to be your man. That's an easy one. You were about to cry over that muthafucka—"

"No, I was—"

"Don't lie," he cut me off, his voice not rising in volume, but a hint of steel entered it, and I found myself doing exactly what he ordered—stop lying. "I saw it all over your face. And if I did, I know your ex did. And he was getting ready to go in for the kill. That's what weak pieces of shit do. Wait until someone is down before attacking. It's the only way they feel powerful or important. And he wasn't doing that bullshit in front of my face. And not to you."

"Why do you care?" For the life of me, I can't figure out the answer to that. I mean, yes, I'm Lennon's best friend, but he doesn't know me. Not for real. We've been in the same room a handful of times, and he's talked to me less than that. "No offense, but you don't look like the Cap'n Save a Ho type."

He barks out a crack of laughter, crossing his arms and pinning a look on me that's somewhere between humor and...something I can't quite decipher. But it has my skin prickling with gooseflesh.

"Did you just call yourself a ho?"

My face balls up, and I flick a hand in his direction. "You know what I mean. I would've never pictured you as the riding to the rescue kind of guy."

"Yeah?" He cocks his head to the side, the corner of that full mouth quirking up at the corner. "Then exactly how do you picture me?"

Naked.

Nope. That shit will not fly out of my mouth. I refuse.

But maybe my face somehow betrays that immediate internal response. Because that half-smile grows into a full smirk, and his green eyes seem to brighten.

Again, nope. This man has pussy thrown at him like it's a national pastime. I'm not reading anything into what *I think* I might see in that damn near glowing gaze.

Clearing my throat, I shrug. And reach for a nonchalance that deserted me the moment he put that lovely, clit-tease of a mouth on mine.

"Honestly?" I ask, answering his very loaded question.

"I practically insist on it."

"You strike me as the 'mind my own business unless it affects me' type."

His dark blond, nearly brown eyebrows almost meet over the bridge of his nose. It's no longer humor flashing in those eyes. Oh no. It's irritation and maybe even embers of anger. His chin tucks toward his neck, and though I'm across the room, he still makes me feel like a specimen pinned to a metal tray with all my organs exposed to the air and him.

"Say again? You take me as some kind of fuck boy that would allow a woman to be disrespected in his face and not do anything about it?"

I consider lying, especially since it seems like I step danced all over his feelings and pride. But let's face it. After tonight, the chances of us having another in-depth conversation are about nil to lottery win, so I might as well be honest. Besides, he insisted on it.

"Not a fuck boy." I shake my head. "But you definitely have a 'you like it, I love it' spirit about you."

His frown deepens. "I have no idea what the fuck that means."

I sigh. "You're not going to step in and get involved in anyone else's shit unless it directly affects you." I hold up my hands, palms out as a rumble rolls out of him. "Sorry! You asked for honesty. But that said, we've barely said more than five words to each other before tonight. So I can be mistaken for my assumption."

"You damn right you're mistaken. My mother would have my ass if I didn't check a man for even raising his voice at a woman."

"Seriously?" I blink. "You sound a bit scared of your mother."

He snorts. "Hold up there, shorty. I'm not scared of anyone. I just have a healthy respect for the woman."

Shorty.

My stomach should not flutter at the sound of that throwaway endearment. Shouldn't. But it certainly does.

To cover my unfortunate reaction, I part to my lips

to tell him I call bullshit, but instead, "Why'd you call me that?" comes out.

Goddammit. My mouth has zero chill or control.

His frown slowly clears, and that sexy smirk makes another appearance. Usually, I find men who smirk a level above douche canoes. But on one Kade Gibson? It now could be in the running for my favorite expression.

"Because you're vertically challenged."

Now it's my turn to be offended. And my outraged gasp clearly conveys my opinion on the subject.

"Excuse you. I'm average height. Did it ever occur to you that you're abnormally tall?" Not for a throwback to a Scandinavian seafarer, but still.

"No, didn't occur to me at all."

I don't know. I'm beginning to think him ignoring me might've been a blessing in disguise.

He uncrosses his arms and curls his fingers around the edge of the desk, and the intensity returns to his stare, all traces of humor fleeing from his sharply honed face.

"Because it looked like you needed a friend."

"Huh?" Not the most intelligent of responses but forgive me. I'm confused.

"The answer for why I brought you in here." He dips his chin. "Because in that moment, you looked like you were lost, alone. And you needed a friend."

If I thought that whole shitshow with Ben had been humiliating, I seriously underestimated how low my bar could go. Because now, sitting here and listening to him describe me as lonely and lost, my mortification exceeded anything Ben could ever inflict. He might as well have called me pathetic. In this moment, I am that. I'm the proverbial puppy bracing itself for a kick to the flank.

And in this moment, I almost hate Kade for it.

I shoot to my feet, my fists riding the sides of my thighs.

"I have enough friends, thank you." I stalk toward the closed office door. "Again, thank you for the save back there. But Lennon is probably looking for me. I should go."

A gentle, but firm grip encircles my lower arm. The touch of calloused, warm skin against mine draws me to a halt faster and harder than the strength of the hold on me. A surge of electrical pulses jolts through me, and I wage a full campaign against the moan rushing from the back of my throat.

"Where you going?"

My lashes flutter closed at that low, sin-wrapped-in-corruption voice. No wonder he doesn't lead any songs for Bloody Sunday. It's a weapon—a siren call that would wreak lust-infused havoc and mayhem. His lips brush again the rim of my ear, and I would love to say my body didn't give a fully body shiver. God, I'd love to be able to claim that—but I can't. And I'm sure he not only saw my reaction to him but felt it. Tack on more embarrassment, please. Because apparently, I haven't met my quota for the week.

"Kade—"

"Was that you trying to dismiss me?" He presses closer, and his wide chest more than spans my back, and *holy shit*. It's been a long time, but I know a dick when I feel it. And a very hard, very *large* dick is nudging the bottom of my spine. "It was cute, but it's also not happening. And, Lena?"

"Yes?" The answer shudders from between my lips on a trembling, soft breath.

I squeeze my eyes tighter.

I'm shameless. I'm sad. I'm greedy and burning

with the hunger rendering me to ash. Forget Lot and his pillar of salt wife. I'm a pillar of lust.

"You can never have too many friends." Before I can reply or protest—and I'm not a hundred percent certain I would have—he turns me around and leads me back to the couch. He gently shoves me down to the cushions then sinks down beside me. "Now your turn to answer a question for me. Why do you believe you don't deserve me showing up for you?"

"I don't—" But I don't need him to cut my lie off this time. I do it myself. Sinking my teeth into my bottom lip, I keep my gaze focused straight ahead, staring at the far wall. "I don't need your pity," I grind out.

"And you don't have it. Look at me, shorty." He pinches my chin and turns my face back toward him. "Ready to answer my question?"

"I..." I try to push the words past the constriction in my throat. But I can't. The truth is like peeling my skin back and exposing every flaw and insecurity to his scrutiny. And I'm terrified of what he'll see.

Hell, I'm terrified of what *I* see.

His hand shifts from my chin, brushing down my neck and collarbone to settle between my breasts. My heart takes off like a convict on a jail break. Surely, he feels the frantic pulse beneath his palm. Part of me wants to knock him away. But the other half... I briefly close my eyes. The other half yearns to press that big, surprisingly gentle hand closer. To hoard that strength he radiates. But it would be a mistake to indulge in it, in him. Because I've learned all too well that it can be snatched away at any second with no warning. The only person I can rely on is me.

"Stop overthinking. Breathe deep, shorty," he murmurs, and I do. I inhale a breath, hold it in my lungs, and then slowly release it. "There you go. Again." He waits for me to comply. Finally, I lift my lashes and meet his gaze again. "Just talk. Don't worry about how it comes out, how I'll take it. Don't worry about being right or wrong. Just talk. Give me what's inside you, and I promise you, Lena, you'll be safe with me."

He can't know that. Can't promise that.

But the lure of that invitation warms me like the rays of a summer sun. And though I know it's foolish and reckless, I give in. Who am I kidding? If he betrays this truth, uses it against me, I will be crushed. Yet... Something inside me urges me to take this small risk. Even if it's just for myself.

But when I part my lips to speak, nothing emerges.

Kade gives his head a small shake, then while keeping his hand centered on my chest, he lifts his other hand and cups the shaved side of my head. He shifts closer to me, and at the same time, he brings me to his broad, hard chest, cushioning my cheek against the wide plane of muscle. Of their own volition, my arms wind around his torso, my fingers splay wide over his back.

"Go ahead," he softly says.

I'm not a child. Yet, inhaling his potent wood and whiskey scent—and his hands on me—cracks open a door that I've shut and sealed closed with crazy glue.

And my darkest, most hurtful truth comes barreling out.

"It's not that I believe I didn't deserve you interfering and stepping up for me tonight. Or maybe I..." The words dry up on my tongue, because even admitting that to myself, much less voicing it aloud seems a bridge too far. And one I can't ever recross. "It's just maybe this is karma or the consequences I have to face. My dad used to say, some sins you can't outrun, you just have to outlive. And Ben…"

"Ben was a mistake. You're allowed to make them just like we all are. Ain't none of us perfect, shorty."

My fingers curl into his shirt, balling the material in my fists.

"I know. I probably knew the moment he started coming at me about my lack of ambition. I believe his exact words were, I'm an ambition succubus, and that my lack of motivation was bringing him down both emotionally and professionally. Apparently, choosing to just be a school secretary instead of pursuing a 'real' career is an anathema to him. Not to mention negatively reflects on him." I pause, all the times he denigrated my intelligence and job rolling through my head like end of movie credits. "I knew when he began staying later and later at his office and talking to me less and less. I ignored all the red flags. I willingly turned a blind eye to all the signs until he shoved the truth in my face with a Dear John letter."

He stiffens against me.

"You mean to tell me, he broke up with you by—"

I nod. "By a letter left on the dining room table."

"What a coward." His mouth firms, and if Ben was here now, I would fear for his safety. Maybe. "Were you working as an administrative assistant when he met you?" I nod, and his full lips curl in a sneer. "Then what's his complaint? Your job is your choice. Do you want to change careers?"

I shrug, grappling with telling him another truth. One I haven't even shared with Lennon. But we're here, and it seems I'm in a confessional mood, so…

"I enjoy working in the elementary school's front office. Sometimes the parents are a pain in the ass, but I love the kids and most of the teachers and administration. Still..." I hesitate. "Still, I've been looking into returning to college for my Masters."

"In?"

"Library Science."

His head jerks back. "You want to be a librarian?"

"I have my bachelor's in it, and at one time I did. But who knows?" I shrug again.

"If that's what you want, what's stopping you?"

I snort. "Some of us aren't millionaires like present company, rock star." His eyes narrow on me, but I wave my hand. "Anyway, you haven't heard the best part of my story." Best. Worst. Absurdity is, after all, in the eye of the beholder. "Ben was so disgusted by my lack of professional drive that he quit his own accountant job and took off to Alaska to fulfill his life-long dream of becoming a crab fisherman in the Bering Sea."

"Nope. Nope nope nope." Kade slides his fingers through my locs, gripping them and tilting my head back and away from his chest. He peers down at me, surprise flickering in his wide eyes. "Did you just tell me he pulled a *Deadliest Catch*? You shitting me?"

A reluctant smile curves my mouth.

"No." I shake my head. "He left. And a couple of months later, returned home. The dream was very short-lived."

He snickers. Then he tips his head back, a deep bellow of laughter rolling out of him.

"Of all the things I expected to come out of your mouth, that wasn't it. Damn." Another crack of humor fills the office, and for a moment, the heaviness in me lifts.

Because, c'mon. It's ridiculous. Just imagining Ben on a crab boat... Yeah, I've had months to try and picture it and that image still eludes me.

But then I remember what came after, and my smile ebbs. After a moment, Kade tips his head back down and his hilarity subsides as his gaze narrows on me.

"What just happened?" he demands. "Something just went through those pretty eyes. Tell me about it."

His hand shifts from my chest to my hip, holding me in place. Holding me against him.

"With Ben, I became someone I didn't recognize. And then the way he left..." I sink my teeth into my bottom lip hard enough to cause a flare of pain. I welcome it, focus on it rather than the humiliation that trips over my skin like a thousand bee stings. "I was so angry. Felt so abandoned and powerless. By the time he returned to town, everyone knew happened. You've no doubt already discovered how it is in a small town. Everybody is nose deep in everyone else's business. So when Ben came home, he wasn't treated to the scrutiny—I was. It seemed like everyone asked what *I did* to make Ben leave the way he did. I felt defective while he just returned and jumped back into life and a new relationship like he hadn't left me ashamed and broken."

"Lena..."

"I threw a dog shit Molotov cocktail on his porch," I blurt out.

For the second time in minutes, he appears stunned. He blinks and his jaw moves, clenches.

Then, "Repeat that, please?"

"To be specific, I threw a flaming bag of dog shit on his porch."

I wait for his response, but his face doesn't lose the slack look of shock. Seconds later, a snicker echoes in the room. Followed by another one. Then another. And then Kade falls back against the couch, holding his stomach as huge guffaws escape him. For a couple of minutes straight, he rocks back and forth, and damn. Are those tears?

I wish I could find it funny. Really do. It would be so much easier if I did. But I can't.

"Are you finished?" I ask, and yes, I have *tone*.

Rolling his lips together, he slides me a side glance. Then falls apart again.

"Kade," I snap.

"Sorry, sorry." He pops a hand up, palm out. Possibly warding off anymore shit-related stories. "I'm good now." Swiping the heels of his palms over his eyes, he clears his throat, but that wide grin remains. "Please. Go 'head."

"It isn't funny."

"The hell it ain't." When I just stare at him, he slowly sobers, that bright gaze roaming over my face. "Shorty," he murmurs. "You set a bag of shit on fire. Personally, I think the symbolism is pretty accurate. If you're expecting judgment from me, it's going to be a long ass wait. You don't want to know all the shit I've done—will probably still do at some point in the future. What's bothering you so much?" He frowns. "You're not upset about *him*, are you?"

I shake my head, rubbing a hand over the shaved side of my head.

"No, of course not. I stopped worrying about and caring for him when he couldn't afford me the same courtesy." I sigh, and my shoulders start to drop, curving forward. But I deliberately straighten them— and look away from Kade. I'm a cornucopia of contradictions. "It's about me. How I let myself get to the point where I committed a misdemeanor. How for so long, I invested 100% of myself in him and our relationship when he didn't even put up a stake in it. I hate myself for that. For staying so long. For being so blind. For losing my voice. No, not losing my voice. Willingly silencing it. I—"

"Don't do that." At his quiet yet flinty tone, I snap my lips closed. "Don't you dare do that. Most of us have been in bad relationships and survived them battered, bruised and with scars. That's life. We learn from them and move the fuck on. And part of moving on is letting shit go. Yeah, you let anger control your actions. Will that happen again? Probably, because you're human. Will you throw flaming shit at a door like a Fourth of July firecracker. No, you won't. You've learned from that. Forgive yourself."

"But most people won't end up a criminal after a break-up."

"Were you arrested?"

I wave my hand. "That's not the point—"

He arches an eyebrow. "Shiiit, speaking as someone who has a record, it's an important point."

"No, it's—seriously? You have a record?" I lean back, squinting at him. "What for?"

"Nah, shorty. This about you." He shakes his head, the corner of his mouth twitching. "All I'm saying is, your *alleged*—" I snort, and his mouth curves into another of those sexy smirks, "—misdemeanor is a life lesson. So is Ben. Next time you get in a relationship, you'll recognize the early signs of a narcissistic piece of shit and get out sooner. Take the lesson, forgive yourself and move on. Not to mention, the asshole I met tonight isn't worth this emotional flagellation. Trust me. He's not beating himself up over how he wronged you. Don't give him any more of your energy."

I stare at him, absorbing his speech. Does it immediately absolve me of my guilt and embarrassment?

No. But my chest isn't as tight, my skin not as hot. And that snarled ball of shame that seemed to take up permanent residency in my belly? It's a little less tangled.

"Thank you," I murmur.

He huffs out a chuckle. "Why do I feel like I surprised you? Again."

"Well..." I shrug and he softly laughs again. "You have to admit, nothing in our previous encounters prepared me for you going Iyanla Vanzant on me. Not that I'm complaining, but it's just...unexpected."

"Y'know, I can be pretty introspective when I'm not drumming or fucking."

Umm.

I should say something flippant here. Something incredibly witty and maybe even a little flirty. But at those incendiary words, my brain has decided to wave the white flag and surrender to the hot need pouring through my body like a swollen flood. Come to think of it, there's another thing that's swollen and wet about me.

Time to go.

Yep. Time to go before I thoroughly embarrass myself by throwing my body over his and finding out for my own information if that dick is as big and good as rumored.

I pinch the bridge of my nose, and after a second, lower my hand and lift my lashes.

And God, I wish I'd left them lowered.

Kade's eyes gleam like jewels, and suddenly I am sympathetic to the fly caught in a spider's web. I'm stuck, unable to move. And all I can do is stare as his gaze drops to my mouth and his tongue makes a brief appearance to lick his bottom lip before he catches it between his teeth.

"I bet you can't lie for shit, shorty," he rumbles,

those damn near fluorescent eyes meeting mine again. "Your face reveals everything you're thinking."

Oh damn, I hope not.

Get up, woman. Get up and walk right out that door now.

Instead, I ask, "What am I thinking?"

The question is akin to striking a match while standing in a pool of gasoline. I'm playing with fire and courting an explosion. Yet, I can't look away. Can't retreat. No, I shift closer to imminent destruction, and I don't care. Excitement races through my veins, not fear, not caution. My lips tingle with the memory of his covering mine. My throat heats, tightens as if his hand once against circles it. I fist my hands down by my thighs so I don't brush my fingertips over my skin.

"Fucking, Lena. You're thinking about me fucking." He cocks his head. "How I fuck. How I'd fuck you." He reaches across the short space separating us and dips his fingers in the top of my dress, grazing the insides of my breasts as he hooks the material and draws me closer. "Tell me I'm wrong."

You're wrong. You couldn't be more wrong.

I shake my head.

Even as my sense of self-preservation throws me a dirty look, that side of me that's so hungry, so greedy to be touched as I haven't been in months does jazz kicks.

A fool? Wreckless?

I could be accurately tagged with those labels. And one more can be tacked on.

Glutton.

For punishment, for lust, for his touch. For *him*.

"Is this what we're doing, little Lena?" He tugs me even closer until our noses almost bump. Until I can taste a hint of the smoky and sweet alcohol he was drinking earlier. "Because you're looking at me like you want my mouth on you and my dick in you."

I shiver, and the groan I try to lock down sneaks out of me like a dirty thief.

"Oh it's like that, shorty?" He hums, dipping his head and dragging his nose down my throat, then retracing the path with his lips.

I squeeze my thighs against the deep ache in my pussy pulsing like a beacon. His hand slides free of my dress, and he shifts it to cup the back of my neck, his thumb rubbing up and down the front of my throat.

His mouth grazes over my cheek, and then he nips the corner of my mouth. My belly quivers, bottoms out. I never realized how empty I was until this moment.

He cradles my face with both hands, tipping my head back.

"Tell me what you want from me?" he growls the demand. "And use verbs."

"Kiss me again. Put your hands on me." I shove out a shaky breath and tremble as if I'm hovering over the edge of a great precipice. In a way, I am. And I leap. "Fuck me, Kade."

Apprehension twists in my belly at the fierce, nearly savage look that passes over his features. Those beautiful, narrowed eyes seem brighter against the stark angles that appear sharper, his mouth fuller. My pussy clenches, spasming around an emptiness that's almost painful with the need to be filled. This is the face of a man who will break me with pleasure. And call me silly or careless, I'm willing to be scattered into pieces.

But then I'm not dwelling on that corkscrew of nerves or how I might not survive this reckless endeavor. I'm not focusing on anything but the claim of my mouth by his. Those demanding lush, yet hard, lips and plunging tongue leave no room for thoughts. Just feelings. And oh God, do I *feel*.

Lust crashes inside me like the cymbals he beats, and I whimper with it. This kiss... Damn. It's different from the one he gave me earlier in the club. That one was sensual, teasing. This one is—in a word—destructive. It's laying waste to me, and I'm rubble at his feet. And each stroke, suck and lick of his tongue rebuilds me.

Tilting my head, I open wider for him, needing more, demanding more. He's giving me what I didn't know I needed tonight. The freedom to get lost. And I'm grabbing ahold of it and him with clasping hands. I'm not letting go until I'm thoroughly fucked and wrecked.

His big hands skate to my head, one cradling my head, and the other tangling in my locs. He drags that beautiful, wild mouth away from mine, and on another whimper that I'll probably be embarrassed about later, I protest, chasing those swollen, damp lips. But he tilts my head down and in a move that steals the little breath remaining in my lungs, he presses a too tender for a one-night-stand kiss to my forehead.

Moisture pricks my eyes, and I circle his thick wrists, holding on for dear life. This caress is a soft whisper in the middle of a chaotic storm. My chest tightens, and a protest crawls up to my throat. I don't want tenderness. I don't want softness. I want raw, primal passion. I want to be taken. Hard.

But I don't pull away. I don't push him away.

And when he scatters gentle, barely there kisses over to my temple, across my cheekbone and down the bridge of my nose, I can't contain the sob that slips past my clenched teeth.

"Shh," he soothes, trailing those butterfly caresses down, skipping my mouth to pepper my jaw. "Get it out so there's no one in this room but you and me."

I did. Later, maybe I would be horrified over crying in this man's arms during a pregame to sex. But there, with his quiet, deep voice murmuring encouragement in my ear, it felt...right. He wouldn't allow me to give my tears to the situation with Ben out there in the club. But here, safe in this office with only him as a witness, he not only encouraged them, but wanted them.

For several minutes, I purge all the anger, hurt and betrayal for the last time. Because from this second on, I'm promising myself that Ben will never receive any more of my time, thoughts or attention. And as I quiet, as the tears ease and eventually subside, his mouth covers mine again.

At first seeking, it evolves into the conflagration and wild need that imbued our previous kiss. I'm like that lit match again, only this time I toss it down to the gasoline and let the flames consume me.

As if the crying unlocked a valve inside me, I fully embrace this passion and crawl onto his thighs, straddling him. I grab the hem of my own dress and tug it up my thighs until it barely covers my ass. The recycled air of the AC system brushes across my exposed skin, and I don't give a damn. Modesty is the first casualty of this lust that sears all of my inhibitions and principles. Besides, with his big hands abandoning my hair and sliding down my back to grasp my ass, I don't feel cold. Oh no, I have a fever raging through me, heating my skin and sending my pulse racing.

This time, it's me who takes control of the kiss. I

mold my lips to his and thrust my tongue inside his mouth, fucking it. I moan as his beards abrades my skin and gliding my palms over the shaved sides of his head, I thrust my fingers in those sexy ass cornrows, digging my fingers in his scalp, scratching it. His growl vibrates against my breasts, and my nipples bead tight as I swallow that dark rumble of sound.

His palms skim over my back and then the sides of my torso. He locates the zipper of my dress and tugs it down until the bodice of my dress sags. I go to free my arms of the off-the-shoulder sleeves, but he doesn't allow it. Dragging his mouth free of mine, he trails his lips down my neck, pausing at my collar bone to lightly bite and suck. But soon he continues farther down, and anticipation and need have my breath escaping me in harsh, quick gasps.

He flicks a glance up at me then lifts his hands and cup my breasts. I cry out, the pleasure and relief of him finally touching me there exquisite and almost too much. Even though my strapless bra still covers me, I swear the heat of his skin burns right through the material.

With abrupt tug, he jerks the bra down, releasing me, and he wastes no time cupping my breasts and pushing them together so my nipples are damn near touching. He growls, the sound dark, greedy, as *finally* he puts his mouth on me. I shudder, another low cry ripping out of me as his tongue licks around one beaded tip and then the other. It's almost gentle, almost a tease. And it's killing me.

Over and over, he continues the torturous pleasure of those lapping licks and playful flicks. My fingers pull on his braids, demanding, pleading for a harder, deeper suck. I part my lips to give voice to that need when he chuckles low in his chest before closing his lips over both painfully tight nipples, pulling them deep into his mouth.

"Oh God," I whine. "Oh fuck."

Lust spasms in my belly and lower in my pussy. Moisture leaks out of me, saturating my thong and no doubt his jeans. I should be embarrassed about that, but later. Right now, I just want more. *More.*

His tongue rolls over the tips, pulling, lashing until he draws another broken, muted scream from me. I lower my hips, seeking out his cock. Needing something to relieve and satiate the hunger tearing through me like a destructive fire. I tilt my head back on my shoulders, giving a long moan as my sex makes contact with that hard, thick length. I don't care that it's covered by denim. I don't give a damn that I'm probably making a mess of both of us. All I care about is the hard, dirty grind over that cock. The bump and slide of it against my clit. The surge of pleasure that drives me closer to orgasm.

"Fuck, you're sensitive," Kade praises, peppering kisses across the top of my breasts. His thumbs circle and flick my nipples, and I twist and rock against him. He's this nasty puppet master and I'm his marionette, dancing to his erotic tune. "I bet you could come just from my mouth on these gorgeous titties. I want to see it, shorty. Let me see it."

It's not a request; he drops one hand to my ass, hauling me upward so my pussy loses contact with his cock.

"No." I try to sink back down, but his grip on my ass tightens, preventing me from lowering again. "I want—"

"Shh." He lifts his hand back to my breasts, holding me up, offering my flesh to him. "I know what you want."

He lowers his head again, and with a muttered curse sucks hard on my nipples again, lapping and tugging at both hardened tips. He's relentless, and when an invisible cord pulls taut low in my belly and a heaviness swells in my pussy, I gasp, and my hips dance to a wild, desperate cadence. I hump air, needing friction, fucking anything to shove me over into release. Then he bites my nipple.

Holy shit.

The scream echoes in my head, not emerging from my parted lips. I stiffen, my pussy spasming hard on a tight, almost painful orgasm. A whine crawls free of me as I shudder, caught between pushing Kade away or holding him closer as he continues to suck and lick, drawing the release out until I slump against him. My breath comes out of me in tiny, explosive puffs against his forehead, and he holds me through every shiver, sweeping his palms up and down my spine.

That orgasm was both a relief and a match to dry kindle. I tug his head back and capture those kiss-swollen, damp lips. My tongue plunges into the depths of his mouth, taking, claiming. We engage in a sensual battle, and like that release, it's pleasure but not enough.

I crawl off his lap and sink to the floor, kneeling between his powerful thighs. He doesn't stop me as I jerk at the button on his jeans, quickly releasing it and jerking down the zipper. I don't hesitate in dipping my hand inside his black boxer briefs. And when I pull him free, for several seconds I just stare at the long, almost brutishly thick cock with the mushroom-shaped head. Pre-cum coated the tip, and nothing could keep me from tasting it, tasting him. His slightly salty, delicious musk explodes on my tongue and suddenly I'm ravenous for more. For all of him.

"Goddamn." He hisses his hands gripping my head, fingers tunneling through my locs. "Don't play with me, shorty. Suck it."

I part my lips, swallowing him, damn near close to another release as his dick slides over my tongue, filling my mouth. A searing hot curse rumbles from him and the muscles in his thighs tauten and tremble around me. Power surges through me, mingling with the pleasure. I did this—I made this beautiful, sexy man quiver. I could get addicted to this.

I wrap my fingers around him, stroking the lower half of his dick that my mouth can't take. My spit and his pre-cum slickens the path, and I jack his flesh while I bob up and down on his dick. I return a hand to his boxer briefs and dip inside, cupping and squeezing his balls, shifting higher on my knees so I can swallow more of him. And when his cockhead nudges the back of my throat, relax, breathe through my nose...take him deeper.

"Fuck yes," he snarls. "Again. Fucking again."

I slide off his cock, swirling my tongue around the tip, then drop down his flesh again, not stopping until he slips inside the channel of my throat. A harsh shout echoes in the room, and then he rips control from me. He tightens his grip on me, holding my head steady for the short, powerful strokes between my lips.

Willingly, I surrender to him, loving every stroke, every second as he uses my mouth in a dirty hand job. His rhythm starts to stutter, and I dig my nails into his denim-covered thighs, waiting for the first hit of his seed on my tongue, down my throat. But it doesn't come.

Kade wrenches me off of him and shoots to his feet. My whine of disappointment is cut short when he drops me on the couch and tears my thong down my legs and tosses it to the floor. My breath abandons me as he reaches into the back pocket of his jeans, removing a condom from a wallet that he also tosses to the floor. Quickly, he shoves his pants down a little lower on his hips, and I'm suddenly struck by the picture we must make.

Me, with my dress bunched around my hips like waist beads, and him fully clothed except for the sag of denim around his ass and thighs. It's raw, it's not gentle or sweet. It's hot, and though I never would've thought this would be me, I'm so fucking glad it is.

Quickly, he sheathes himself, and he lifts his gaze to mine, and I'm scorched by the bright flames there.

"That's such a pretty pussy," he says, voice gravel rough yet, it's almost a purr. I shiver. "You going to let me have it, Lena?"

Oh, hell yes. I'm going to die if he doesn't take it. I nod.

"Unh-unh." He grips the base of that impossibly long cock. "Give me the words. You going to let me sink into this pretty pussy until you take all of it? Every inch of me, Lena. You can't hold out on me. Know what you're agreeing to."

"Yes," I say before he even finishes his sentence— or warning. I'm not entirely sure which one it is. But I want it. I want all of it and him.

"Good, shorty. Good."

He falls over me, one hand presses into the couch cushion above my shoulder and the other stays wrapped around his dick, notching the head at the mouth of my pussy. He pushes forward, and I cry out at the burning sensation of him stretching me wide. On reflex I push against his abdomen, but he swats my hands away, shaking his head.

"Nah, shorty. You promised," he growls, and crouching over me, continues to drive forward.

I twist under him, trapped between nearly painful pressure and mind-numbing pleasure. I'm not used to this overfull sensation or the need that tears at me with greedy talons. It's too much and not enough. It's crazy and utterly sane.

I'm a mess.

I dig my nails into his T-shirt covered back, helplessly holding on as he withdraws and then slides back inside my pussy, a merciless campaign to make me do as he demanded and take all of him. And he accomplishes what he set out to do when his pelvis meets mine, and I'm stuffed full. I squirm beneath him, restless, totally as his mercy and there is no other place I'd rather be.

He stills, granting me time to become used to his possession, but I want none of it. Yes, pain still edges the pleasure, but I want that bite. I want to be fucked like an animal. I want *everything*.

"You good?" He lowers his head, brushes a kiss over my lips and the caress is oddly tender considering what his cock is doing to my pussy.

"Yes," I rasp. "Please. Fuck me. I need—*oh God*."

He pulls free of my pussy and thrusts back inside... hard. And damn, it doesn't seem possible but I'm already rocketing toward another orgasm. I can't contain my shocked cry, and I close my eyes and hold on for this chaotic and wild ride.

Pushing my thighs higher, he fucks me with wild abandon. His thighs slap against the back of mine as he drives in and out of me at a furious, relentless pace.

"Dammit, Lena, look at you. Just fucking look at you taking it. Goddamn, it's so fucking good."

His praise spurs me and my pleasure on, and

damn, who knew that was my kink? Dirty talk and praise, but only with him.

And shit, is that a dangerous thought.

It's because I'm incoherent with the ecstasy threatening to tear me apart. That's the reason ideas of "only" are tripping through my head. And as the need coalesces in a tight, hard knot, I scream, my hips twisting, surging, seeking...

Another scream erupts from me as that knot unfurls and explodes into a white hot ball of fire, hurling me into a release that both frightens and exhilarates me.

"Shit. *Shit.*" Kade slams into me again and again, then on a long and deep groan, stiffens above me.

His cock throbs as he releases, and I slowly sink into a peaceful oblivion, absorbing each shudder and jerk of his body. Kade sags forward and I rub my hands over his back, closing my eyes, smiling at his low grunts and harsh puffs of breath caressing my neck.

I fucked this man in the office of a club. And tomorrow—hell, an hour from now—I might have regrets. But not now.

Not now.

2

Kade

Goddammit.

I bow my head, pinching the bridge of my nose and cursing again.

"Shit," I growl, staring down at the cream colored invitation with its dark green lettering. This is what I get for letting people know where I live.

And by "people," I mean my family.

Dropping the card on my dining room table, I stalk across the open room layout to the sunken living room, not stopping until I get to the bar. I grab a decanter of whiskey and splash two fingers in a thick, glass tumbler. Without hesitation—or consideration of it being just nine o'clock in the morning—I toss it back, grimacing at the fiery hit. Before it even hits my stomach, I pour more. And repeat. Squinting at the decanter, I consider another shot.

Better not.

Rehearsal is at King's place in another couple of hours. I can't show up drunk off my ass. As much as I would like to find oblivion at the bottom of this bottle, it wouldn't be fair to my bandmates. Especially to

King, who has been kicking sobriety's ass. I wouldn't do that to him.

Sighing, I walk over to one of the floor-to-ceiling windows that comprise three of my four walls. As many times as I question how on earth I ended up in this little backwater town of Pike's End, I can't deny its beauty. Mt. Rainier sits in the distance, its peaks still snowcapped even though it's May. Below, the Puget Sound gleams, and since moving here, I've spent several mornings on my back deck, watching the dawn with a steaming cup of coffee. It's not L.A. or New York, but I suppose it has its own charm. And if I had to settle anywhere, Pike's End isn't the worst option. Still, love brought King here, and friendship brought me, Gideon and Mac. I've yet to feel the pull for this place like my best friend. But... I glance over my shoulder toward the dining room where that invitation sits like a fucking booby trap. But this small town is better—safer—than the city I left behind years ago.

Four years, to be exact.

My fingers clench around the glass, and I stifle the urge to throw it against the far wall.

Dammit. Just a simple card, and already I want to commit violence.

The theme to *Bridgerton* echoes from the kitchen, and though love and a spark of humor blooms in my chest, I still grimace. Since bingeing the popular Netflix series with my mother last year when she came to visit me in L.A., I set that piece of music as her specific ring tone.

Usually, I enjoy speaking with her; I love Charlene Gibson more than any other woman. But right now, suspecting why she's calling...

"Shit."

Spinning on my bare heel, I stride for the kitchen

and the cell that I left on the counter next to the coffee machine. It stops ringing just as I hit the entrance, but seconds later, it starts again. Yeah, there's no avoiding her.

Picking it up, I press the screen and lift the phone to my ear.

"Hey, Ma."

"Hey, how's my baby boy?"

I groan. "Ma, I'm thirty-one." We never fail to have this conversation.

"Thirty-one or one. You will always be my baby. Deal with it." And she never fails to say this either. A reluctant smile pulls at my lips. "Now, you know why I'm calling."

Hitting the speaker button, I lay the phone back on the counter and flatten my palms on the counter. I shake my bowed head, eyes closed.

"Ma..."

"Nope. Not trying to hear it. If you, Kade Theodore Gibson, don't show up at your father and my anniversary party, I will fly all the way to wherever you are and give you an ass whooping that will make the ones from childhood look like pattycake."

"Damn, Ma. Stop with the Theodore." I wince.

"Watch your mouth. And if you don't want me to call you by your name, then stop with the excuses you're about to give me," she snaps, but then her tone softens. "It's our thirty-eighth wedding anniversary. And we would really love if you'd come home for it. Kade, it's been long enough."

No, it hasn't. Forty years wouldn't be enough. But I keep that to myself.

"I haven't forgotten about your anniversary. I already have something planned for you and Dad. As a matter of fact, I was going to call you next week to see if you—"

"Kade."

Just my name in *that* tone, the one that expresses disappointment and love, is enough to shut me down. Clenching my jaw, I reach for the coffee machine and drop a pod of breakfast blend into the top then slap it down.

"Yeah, Ma?"

"It's been four years," she says, echoing my earlier thoughts. "You can't stay away forever. It's time to come home."

Home? Boston hasn't been my home for some time. I left it, the memories and the pain behind with no intentions of visiting any of them again.

"Ma, you and Dad should come visit me here after the party," I try again, punching the power button. In seconds, the hiss of brewing coffee fills the room, followed by the mouthwatering aroma of coffee grounds. "I'm sure you'll be ready for a vacation anyway. You guys can stay a week here then we can travel somewhere else. Like the Bahamas or Fiji. I remember you mentioning several times how you'd like to see—"

"Stop it." She doesn't yell the order, but she might as well have. Once more, I press my palms into the countertop, leaning all of my weight onto them. "You've been running, Kade, and it's gone on too long. I let you do it at first—agreed to come out to wherever you were lying your head at the time if we wanted to see you—but not anymore. I'm asking as your mother to. Come. Home."

"That's not fair," I murmur.

"Life isn't fair, baby boy. If anyone knows that, you do." She sighs, and the heaviness in it weighs on my chest.

This is my mother. My champion. My cheerleader. My friend. She's everything to me, and I would give her the same. But this... *Fuck.* "I've avoided asking you for this, Kade. I wanted you to heal and find peace at your own pace, but you've been stuck. I don't care how old you get; you're still my child and I'm still you're parent. And it's my job to help you become unstuck. You need to come home. Your dad and I need to lay eyes on you. And not on some tropical island, but here. Besides, your father... He's been ill and I'm not comfortable with him traveling so far yet."

Panic and fear blast through me in red hot streaks, and I straighten. Turning, I thrust a hand through my hair, staring blindly down out of the bank of kitchen windows.

"Dad?" I rasp. "What do you mean he's been ill? When? How long? Why didn't either of you say anything before now?"

"He had a coronary event about six months ago."

"Shit. What do you mean a coronary event? Like a heart attack?" My fist tightens in my hair, pulling tight until prickles of pain pepper my scalp.

"Watch your mouth," she admonishes but without heat. "Yes, he had a small heart attack after a golf game. He had to get a stent put in, and he's been fine since. But like I said, I don't want him traveling so far yet. I need about ten years to get over the sight of him collapsing."

"*God.*"

I hadn't been there. I didn't know. *Why didn't I know?*

"Why didn't you tell me? Why didn't he?"

Anger flickers inside me, but I can't ignore that the fire is flamed by my own guilt. Because I can't avoid the truth no matter how much I'd like to. I can't look away from it. If I'd gone home, I would've known. If I wasn't such a fucking coward, I wouldn't have to find out about my father's health months later. I would've been right there by his side.

This is on me, not Ma. Not Dad.

Me.

"We didn't want to worry you, Kade," she softly says. "Especially given everything you, King, Gideon and Mac have gone through this past year. You had enough to deal with, and we decided not to add to that burden."

"Ma, you and Dad could never be a burden. What're you talking about?"

"If it had been more serious, we would've contacted you. But now you do know, and we want to see you at our party. Are you coming home?"

I close my eyes, but the action doesn't block out my mom's words. Or my guilt.

Or my resignation.

"Yeah, Ma. I'm coming home."

I DRUM my fingers against the steering wheel, staring at the front of the elementary school as the last of the staff trickles out the doors. Impatience beats inside me to the rhythm of my fingers. After an hour of sitting in this car, I'm bored as fuck and it's starting to get hot, even with the air conditioning blowing. Or maybe it's the annoying twist of nerves in my stomach.

As a full grown man, it's stupid to be nervous about seeing a woman.

Especially a woman I've seen naked and have been balls deep in.

Doesn't matter that two weeks ago, she damn near rendered me comatose with that sweet, tight pussy that's so good it should be commemorated with a national holiday. Doesn't matter that the sweat was barely dry on our skin before she jumped off my dick and fled out the office. It absolutely doesn't matter that she's been avoiding being in the same room with me since then.

Nope. None of that matters.

Yet, as Lena Graves finally emerges from the building, talking with a slightly shorter woman with thick, dark natural curls, my gut pulls tighter, twists harder.

Shit, I've fucked plenty of women over the years. And though I still wake up from dreams of that night with my fist surrounding my hard, throbbing cock, she's just like the other women. A one night stand. And the anxiety trickling through my veins is due to the purpose of this errand.

Not the woman.

Dammit.

Sighing, I shove open the driver's door and step out of my black 1969 Chevrolet Camaro ZL1. Moving to the rear of it, I lean against the rear side panel, crossing my arms and watching her come closer.

Given why I'm here, I really shouldn't study how the pair of high-waisted red pants cling to her thick, toned thighs and rounded hips, or the way the white, short-sleeved shirt emphasizes the thrust and fullness of her perfect breasts. My memory provides a full Power Point presentation of how that gorgeous, sensitive flesh filled my hands, how those cinnamon colored nipples beaded against my tongue.

Yes, cinnamon.

I might've googled the exact shade of brown.

Fuck. Don't judge me.

Her auburn locs are pulled into a bun on top of her head, revealing both shaved sides of her head and that stunning bone structure that would have a sculptor begging her to be their muse. Retro-style glasses perch on that proud nose with its wide nostrils, and that cock tease of a mouth curls into a smile as her friend demonstrates something with hand gestures. Correction. Not cock tease. Those plush, soft lips fully delivered on their promise.

I shift against the side panel, blood already rushing to my dick at the thought of what those lips could do. Grinding my teeth, I will my steadily hardening flesh to stand down. Now is not the time to brick up. Not when I'm about to proposition her.

As if she feels my attention on her, Lena turns her head in my direction. She jerks to a stop, and though she's still too far away for me to glimpse those lovely hazel eyes, I can just imagine them widening with shock. The same surprised expression that had suffused her face when I first pushed inside her pussy...

Goddammit, stop.

I straighten away from my car, and as if that one motion shatters her immobility, she tears her gaze away from me and returns her focus to her friend. They converse for another few moments, and the other woman glances my way with a slight frown before hugging Lena and striding off across the parking lot. Lena waits for several moments, and then her slender shoulders draw back, and she heads in my direction.

I don't meet her halfway; I remain standing and wait for her to approach me. Not out of arrogance or to exert control. No, it's to grant her the choice of walking away or continuing toward me. There's also the small, insignificant fact that I can't move. Not with images of me clutching those sexy as fuck hips that roll in a natural rhythm. Clutching them and holding her still as I pounded up inside her like my life depended on nutting.

Oh God. This isn't going to work. If I had just an iota of common sense, I would climb in my car now and drive off. Chalk that night in the club office up to a one-off and revert our relationship back to the casual "your best friend dates my best friend" acquaintance status.

But my common sense must be on a baecation with my self-preservation because I don't move. Don't fucking breathe until she's standing in front of me, head tipped back, brown and green eyes fixed on mine.

Why do I feel threatened by a woman that's damn near a foot shorter than me? Why do echoes of panic reverberate through me? Why is my heart inching toward my throat? Thank God, the Camaro is at my back or else I might've retreated. And how embarrassing would that have been?

Fucking very.

"Kade," she says, that husky, sensual voice sliding over my skin like a dirty caress. "What're you doing here?"

"For you." Yeah, I don't like how that came out—or the ambiguity in it. Especially since I'm questioning the meaning behind it myself. "Can I talk to you for a few minutes? I promise not to hold you up too long."

I need to stay focused on why I'm here, and not get sidetracked by my overactive brain. Or that delectable scent that haunts my senses. Vanilla and a creamy, rich aroma that reminds me of rain on a rose petal.

Christ. Somebody stop me. Maybe I should switch up and write more ballads since I'm apparently getting in touch with my emotional side.

Mentally grimacing, I wave toward my car.

"I know you probably want to head home after a day at work. And I won't make this long. But I really... need to speak with you about something." I pause. "Please."

She tilts her head, eyes narrowing. Then she huffs out a dry chuckle. "Please, huh? Why do I feel like you might've strained something adding that word." With another short laugh, she shrugs. "Okay, but all I can give you is about fifteen minutes. I have an appointment to get to."

"I'll take it."

Rounding the rear of the car, I pull open the passenger side door. She stares at me, unmoving for several long seconds. Muttering, "Whatever," she follows me and slides into the seat. I close the door behind her then get inside.

I part my lips, but fuck if I know how to start this conversation. On the way here, I'd rehearsed my proposition, going over my points and any potential arguments she might raise. But now, with her sweet, sultry scent permeating the interior of the Camaro, every word flees, my mind a complete blank.

"It seemed like whatever you wanted to say to me was important," she nudges, shifting and leaning her shoulder against the window. "And I don't have a lot of time, so..."

"Yeah. Sorry." I drag a hand over my braided hair. Clearing my throat, I gather my thoughts. I'm here for one reason, and it's paramount that I accomplish that goal. If not... The "if not" is enough to snatch my focus back on track. "First, I need you to keep an open mind about what I'm about to ask you. Just hear me out, and then once you have, make a decision."

She arches an eyebrow, crossing her arms. "Ooh. Now I'm really intrigued. Okay, I can do that."

"Good. Thank you." Heaving a sigh, I rub my palm over my head again then run it down my beard. "I'm returning home to celebrate my parents' anniversary in a couple of weeks. It's their thirty-eighth, and they're throwing a party with all of our family and friends. My mother personally called to make sure I'm coming home for it."

"That's awesome. Thirty-eight years. They definitely should celebrate such an amazing milestone. I don't know many people who have stayed together that long," she says, then scoffs. "My parents didn't even make it to five."

The urge to dive into that statement and learn more about her tugs so strong, I brace myself against the almost physical ache.

Focus. Focus, dammit.

"Yeah, they're definitely relationship goals. Y'know, if you're into that." Her eyes sharpen, but I ignore that, too. "Anyway, this is where you come in. I can't go home alone, but as you're very aware of, I'm not involved with anyone. So I want you to go with me. It'll be for four days, and I'll pay for everything. Your plane ticket, expenses—"

"Hold up, hold up." She fully turns toward me, waving her hands, palms out. She leans forward, pushing into my personal space, a frown carved into her forehead. "Are you okay? You good? No, I really need to know. Because who asks a woman they barely know to go to their family's home with them on an all-expenses paid trip. And do what? Pretend to be your fake girlfriend?"

She snickers, but when I don't laugh or correct her, those beautiful eyes widen, and she gasps. Falling back against the car seat, she gapes at me. As if emerging from a stupor, she shakes her head.

"You're not serious."

"Oh, but I am."

"No, you're not."

"Yeah, I am."

Closing her eyes, she pinches the bridge of her nose with one hand and presses a hand out toward me with the other.

"Lena."

"Nope. Unh-unh. I'mma need a minute." Blowing out a breath, she opens her eyes, dropping her hands to her lap. "A fake girlfriend," she enunciates. "You know real people don't do this, right? I mean, I don't know. Maybe this is par for the course with rock stars, but people like me? School secretaries? We don't do this shit."

Even though nothing about my current situation is funny, a spurt of humor bubbles up inside of me.

"FYI, rock stars don't usually do this either. At least not the drummers. Now lead guitarists and singers?" I shrug. "They're a different breed."

"Funny. I'm delighted you can find humor while asking me to be your fraudulent significant other." She jerks her chin up. "Explain. And I don't mean the abridged version you just gave me. I want all the information you're *not* saying."

I consider deflecting, telling her there isn't anything else to add. But not only do I have the sense Lena would be able to see right through my bullshit, but there's a part of me—a part I need to see a doctor or exorcist about—wants to tell her the truth. If I expect her to trust me, at least long enough to agree to this...bargain, then I can't lie to her right out the gate.

If only the truth didn't stab a dagger in my heart as well as my back. If only it didn't cast me the fool in this fucking tragedy.

"All right." I rub my palms together then wrap my fingers around the steering wheel as if it's my lifeline. "This anniversary party... It would be the first time I've been home in four years. I've avoided it." I pause, waiting for her to ask the next logical question, but she doesn't. Lena remains quiet, although her sharp gaze is like a palm stroking down my face. "Four years ago, my brother got married, eloped. And it was with the woman I believed was my fiancée."

"Holy shit," she breathes.

I bark out a crack of laughter, but there's nothing humorous in it. At least the sound isn't as bitter as it once was.

"Yeah, it's a cliché, really. Fall in love, believe the woman I'm with understands and accepts that my career takes me on the road often. Woman grows discontent and cheats. Only usually, that other person isn't a relative."

"That's fucking low. I don't know your brother, but that's some snake shit and family doesn't do that to one another. Even my fath—" she frowns, then pops up a finger. "Nope. He'd totally do that. Which just proves my point that your brother's on some snake shit."

I blink. And the corner of my mouth quirks in a small half-smile.

"Are you offended on my behalf, shorty?"

Her expression abruptly clears, going blank and *dammit*. I didn't mean to drag reminders of our night together into this conversation. That kind of sexual tension, that kind of need can have no place here between us.

That still doesn't stop me from dropping my gaze to her mouth. Doesn't prevent me from picturing them swollen from the fucking we called a kiss. From seeing those pretty, lush lips stretched wide around my cock...

Clenching my teeth, I force back the tidal wave of lust that slams into me, rattling my bones. Seconds of taut silence hum in the car, and I quietly inhale a deep breath, clearing my head of everything but the plan. It's all about the plan.

"I would be offended and disgusted on behalf of anyone who was betrayed like you were," she says.

"Thank you for that, but there's no need. It's been four years, and I'm over it."

"Umm, okay. If you were over it, you would've been home before now, but I'mma let you have that for the sake of argument."

"Now, you're sounding like my mother." And they were both wrong.

"She sounds like a wise woman. I like her already. *Not*," she jabs a finger at me, "that I'm agreeing this inane idea of yours. Okay, another question. Why me? You being," she draws a circle in front of my face, "*you* should have plenty of women to choose from who would love to be your woman. And if I remember correctly, you told me I can't lie for shit. So why bring this to me?"

"That right there," I say. "Women who would love to be my woman, and wouldn't be able to separate pretend from reality. At the end of the trip, I don't want to have that kind of hassle on my hands. We had sex and you didn't get clingy. Hell, you scraped me off. I don't have to worry about you catching feelings. But besides that, you're beautiful. Smart. Articulate. And we obviously have chemistry so that will be believable. You're the perfect person for this."

Not to mention, while she might be done with her ex, he'd hurt her too bad for her to be willing to enter another relationship anytime soon. That much was obvious from that night.

"How're you willing to lie to your family about this, though? I'm not fully understanding why you need a plus one—oh wait. Let me guess." She wrinkles her nose. "You're still in love with your brother's wife and need me as a beard."

My own bearded chin jerks towards my neck. Is she shitting me?

"What?" I give my head a hard shake. "No. Fuck no. I wouldn't touch her with your bitch ass ex's dick much less still have love for her. But you're half right. Well, almost. I need you as a buffer, not a beard. There's something else," I hesitantly confess.

"There's more?" She looses a dry chuckle. "Goddamn, Kade, this is some next level *Young and the Restless* shit. You're making it real difficult to say yes."

"Yeah, I'm getting that." I didn't want to divulge this part of the story, but here we are. "I've let go of Mira, but she hasn't gotten the memo. I think because I haven't been in a relationship since I found out about her and my brother, she takes that as a sign that I'm still in love with her. Last year, she started texting me. And when I blocked her, she slid into my DMs. I do the same thing—block her—and she creates another account to contact me. She's fucking relentless."

Lena gasps, her fingers flying to the base of her throat. "Shut. The. Whole. Front. Door." When I don't reply, her mouth firms, nostrils flaring. "I can't believe the nerve—have you told your brother?"

I'm shaking my head before she even finishes asking the question. "No. One, he probably wouldn't believe me, even with the evidence of her messages. He'd be more likely to believe I messaged myself, pretending to be her to get revenge rather than accept that he's married to a scheming bitch. And two, as much as I hate what the both of them did, I don't want to be the cause for them ending their marriage."

"From the sound of it, they have problems and it's more than you."

I shrug. "Possibly. But it's not my business. And I don't want it to be. I just want to go, get through this party and leave. Lena." I start to reach for her, but at the last moment flatten my hand on the seat. "I know I'm asking a lot of you. But I'll pay you for the days you have to take off work along with all travel and expenses while we're there. Also," I pause, because damn, this could go wrong, no matter my intentions, "when we were...together, you mentioned wanting to return to school. If you agree to do this with me, I'll pay for your tuition for the master's program. Completely."

Her body stiffens, and tension practically radiates from her.

Damn.

"I'm not a whore," she snaps.

"I didn't mean—"

"It's one thing to offer to pay for my travel expenses. It's quite another to pay thousands of dollars in tuition. Just what the fuck do I have to do to earn that?"

"Lena, nothing, I swear. No strings. No sex. And the only touching is what will be required to pull off this charade. But I won't cross any boundaries you set." This time I reach across the space separating us and take her hand. Though hers remains slack in mine, she doesn't snatch her arm back either. "Listen, you're helping me. I get to go home for the first time in years, and hopefully be able to focus on just my parents without the bullshit and drama that my ex will no doubt try to stir. I just want any measure of peace in a situation that's already going to be awkward. Peace doesn't have a price tag, so offering to pay for this program is the least I can do. And not to brag, but shorty, the cost of your tuition is pocket change."

Slowly, the rigidity eases from her frame, and she glances away from me. But I can still see her chewing on her full bottom lip. It takes everything in me not to offer my services in doing that for her. I remember the taste and texture of that lip, of that mouth.

I release her hand and lean back against my door, inserting more space between us.

"That didn't sound arrogant at all," she mutters, but the heat, the hurt that threaded through her voice just moments ago have disappeared. She sighs, rubbing a hand over her head. I noticed that tell at the club. I wonder if she even realizes she does it.

"I can't believe I'm even saying this but..." Lena huffs out a breath, looking back at me. "Fine. I'll do it."

"Damn, shorty. Thank—"

"Not so fast. I have conditions." She holds up a hand, cutting off my gratitude. But she can't stem the relief flooding through me. Conditions? I'd agree to give her anything she asked for right now. "One, I'm good with PDA as long as we have an audience. But when we're not in front of your family, you need to respect my personal space."

"Bet."

"Two, this...arrangement stays between us. King's your friend and Lennon's mine, but I don't want either one of them knowing about it."

I frown, feeling some kind of way about her wanting to keep any association with me a secret, but after a moment, I nod. Whatever. It just goes into the vault along with that night in the office.

"And three, I'll let you pay my tuition. But I'm paying you back."

"No, I insist—"

"No, *I* insist. It will be a loan and I'll start paying you back six months after I graduate in monthly installments. That should be long enough for me to find a new position. It's not up for discussion and is my deal breaker."

The firm set of her lips and the subtle thrust of her chin informs me there's no changing her mind.

"Fine. But the loan will be interest free." When her eyes narrow behind her glasses, I cock my head and extend my hand toward her. "That's non-negotiable. Deal?"

She studies my hand for several long seconds—long enough for me to question if this is the hill she's willing to die on. But then she slips her hand in mine, curving her fingers around mine.

"Deal."

Looks like my plan is coming together, and I have a pretend girlfriend.

What could possibly go wrong?

3

Lena

"I think you left out some important information when you told me about your family," I mutter, gazing out the rear window of the town car at the stately brownstones with their dark shutters and vibrant flower boxes. Gaslit streetlamps dot the sidewalks, and it's like I've stepped back in time to a long ago age of horse drawn carriages and...Revolutionary War.

I've never been to Boston before, much less the historic neighborhood of Beacon Hill, but I don't need previous experience or a tour book to point out that this area is affluent. Like posh, *I can trace my ancestors back to the Mayflower* affluent. Like, forty-eleven different kinds of forks at the dinner table affluent.

Oh yeah, Kade omitted some minor details, all right.

The key one being he came from money.

Of course, I've known all along that the man is richer than Midas and his Uncle Harry. But I assumed that wealth originated from being a member of one of the most popular rock bands on the globe. And even then, if not for that muscle car that bore a hefty price tag—nine hundred thousand. Hell yeah, I looked it up!—and his big farmhouse of a home, he doesn't flaunt his money. T-shirts, jeans, leather jackets and boots. That encompassed the wardrobe I'd seen grace his tall, big body. Accompany it with a mouth that would make a sailor clutch their pearls and a body that fucked like it'd invented the damn thing, he was surprisingly laid back and without airs.

But now...

I slide a glance over at him.

Now, he's nearly this stranger I don't recognize. A black suit that's obviously custom made as it fits his big frame immaculately. A crisp white dress shirt that's left open at the throat—and okay, I might've stared at that golden, delicious triangle of exposed skin a little too long when he first stepped out of his penthouse bedroom—and stretches over his chest and abs like a level ten clinger who just hasn't got the memo. Instead of battered boots, a shining pair of black shoes that probably has an Italian name. Thank God for the colorful tattoos that climb up his throat or I might have thought a body snatcher had been at work.

Most unrecognizable of all, though? His leg jumping about a hundred miles a minute. I've known no one but the confident, easy-going drummer. Even when he had me in his car asking me to go along with this charade, he exuded a self-assurance that's as hot as fuck as it is annoying. But this obvious display of nerves? I don't know this person.

The only familiar things about him are his beard and hair. The thick facial hair still covers his jaw and surrounds his mouth, but the braids are gone. And the golden strands on his head are slicked back into a low bun.

While this glossier version of Kade is still beautiful, I kind of prefer the scruffier, Viking-esque one. Only because the latter is more genuine. More *him*. The suit, shoes, hair—they seem like armor he's strapped on in preparation for Armageddon. Elegant, expensive armor, but still…

Armor.

Swallowing a sigh, I reach out and lay a hand on his knee. The jittery movement ceases and his head whips toward me, those bright green eyes hitting me like high beams.

"It's going to be okay," I murmur.

"The girlfriend act doesn't start until we're in front of my family."

I clench my teeth against the sharp retort that sits like a red-hot knife on my tongue. Usually, he would've been checked—Ben dented my gansta, but Kade shouldn't get it twisted that I'm a fucking doormat to let anyone talk to me sideways.

But I also know where that heat came from. His leg might've stopped its drum solo, but tension stretches his body so tight, one strong blow from the air conditioning vent could snap him in half.

He better be glad I'm empathetic.

"I'mma let you have that one because of the circumstances. But it's only going to be that one. Yeah, you're essentially paying for me to be here, but I will walk."

His jaw jumps under the dark blond hair, but a moment later, he blows out a loud breath. And his hand covers mine, gently squeezing.

"I'm sorry. You didn't deserve that. Not when you're doing me a favor." Giving my hand another quick squeeze, he then shifted it to his thigh, where his fingers tapped out a soundless rhythm. "I'm nervous."

"You don't say." A wry ghost of a smile twisted his lips. I clap my hands and rub them together. "Okay, while we still have a little time, let's recap our love story again."

He arches an eyebrow. "Love story?"

"Of course." I scoff. "Didn't you know it's epic? World famous rock star takes one glance across a packed stadium—"

"I thought it was King's living room."

"Eh." I flick a hand. "Tomato, to-mah-to. Anyway, one glance and you *had* to know who this ravishing creature was." I ignore his snort. "You begged King for an introduction, and though he—"

"Begged? Shorty, I don't beg."

"Was reluctant to do so," I continue, talking over him, "because I was his girlfriend's best friend, he caved. Because you wouldn't be naysayed."

"Naysayed?"

"Once we were introduced, we spent the entire evening talking. You immediately found yourself captivated by my beauty. I mean, who wouldn't? I'm a snack." I wave my hand in front of me. "But my wit also made me irresistible. And though I had concerns because you're *you*, I still gave us a chance, and for the last six months, we've been inseparable."

He slow claps, and I dip my head in an abbreviated bow.

"Now I know why you're going for your masters in library sciences. You love being around and reading books. Fantasy being the primary genre."

I bite down on my lower lip, stifling the grin that threatens to break free.

"Well, it's better than the story you came up with," I point out, squinting at him.

He shrugs. "What? We met at a club, fucked and it's history from there."

I roll my eyes. "See, what not's going to happen is having your parents—especially your mom—think I'm a groupie with an extended expiration date."

"Groupie? My story just says we have chemistry. And honestly, it's more believable than yours."

"See?" I jab a finger at him. "That's why mine is better because it's not your usual M.O. Nope, we're going with mine. I hope you took notes."

"Don't worry about me, shorty. I'll hold down my end of this. Can you?"

"Please." I wave off his question. "I was damn near a theater major. If I can nail Elle Woods, then playing your girlfriend is not a problem."

"Wait." He cocks his head, and a smile slowly stretches his mouth. "Elle Woods as in *Legally Blonde*?"

"The musical, too." I buff my nails on my off-the-shoulder sleeve. "Are you impressed? You sound impressed. As you should be."

He chuckles, and the sound rolls over my skin in a delicious caress. I fight back a shiver. This is business. Yes, we had an, um...physical encounter, but that was in the past. We're strictly employer, employee. And if the thought of that leaves a faint trail of grime under my skin, well, there are times in life when we do what we have to do in order to meet the end goal.

What's the end goal for me? To shut certain people up. Ben. My father. Even though my father never met a zipper he didn't lower or a skirt he didn't lift, he still has time to criticize my life. He's a rich, successful attorney in Seattle, and like Ben, he couldn't understand why I choose to be an administrative assistant. He complains about the money he spent on my college tuition only for me to be "somebody's secretary." Dad's words, not mine.

I shouldn't care what either him or Ben think about me; neither one pays my bills or have contributed to my life in any meaningful way. But... I can't lie and claim that me wanting to return to school for my master's doesn't have anything to do with them. To prove to them that I'm just as smart as them, just as driven, just as *good*. What does it say about me that I'm willing to spend thousands of dollars on a degree as one big Kiss My Ass?

Not anything good. And yet, here I am, in this limo with a man who's willing to pay my tuition so he can fend off his ex's unwanted advances and convince his parents he's happy.

We're both liars.

"We're here."

The tension invades his frame again and his voice flattens.

Turning back to the window, I gasp at the huge, elegant brick home with its arched, red door and gaslit sconce hanging down over it. How a McMansion can be charming, I don't know, but it is. Maybe it's the large plants on stone pedestals, spilling their long branches and leaves nearly to the ground. Or it could be the roses in the flower boxes at the bottom of the black-shuttered windows. Maybe even the twinkle of white fairy lights entwined around the iron railings on either side of the short flight of steps. Whether it's one of those details or all of them, the home is beautiful and welcoming.

"You grew up here?" I ask, awed.

My father is a wealthy man, but even his sprawling

home in the affluent neighborhood of Broadmoor doesn't touch this.

"Yes. You ready?" He's already pulling on the handle and pushing the door open before the driver can get out.

Seconds later, he opens mine as well, holding a hand out to me. Making sure I don't Britney Spears him, I swing both of my legs out of the car and let him pull me to my feet.

"I'll give you a call when we're ready to go," he tells the driver, who nods and returns to the front seat. Exhaling a heavy breath, he settles a hand on the middle of my back and guides me up the steps to the front door.

"I repeat," I mutter, "You left out some important details about your family."

"They're a family like any other."

"Sure," I drawl, and glance down at myself.

The flirty, light blue, off-the-shoulder puff sleeve dress with its bell shape and the wraparound stiletto heels seemed appropriate and perfect when I put it on. But now? On the stoop of a house that belonged in Architectural Digest?

"You look beautiful. Stop it."

I tip my head back, meeting his steady gaze.

"Thank you." I nod. "Let's do this."

"Finally, I get the miracle worker alone."

I smile at Tracey, Kade's sister. The statuesque woman is a feminine version of Kade. Tall. Blonde. Beautiful with those killer cheekbones, eyes and mouth. But after meeting Charlene and Mason, their parents, I can see from where they inherited their features. Kade and Tracey are a perfect combination of those two. If not for how incredibly—and surprisingly—gracious and down-to-earth they all were, I would probably be hating on them. Rich, gorgeous and successful? Like, God, leave some for the rest of us.

But regardless of this house with its floor-to-ceiling windows, high ceilings, curved stairwell, cavernous fireplaces and richly appointed furniture, they are as laid back as Kade. Well, how Kade usually is, anyway.

I cut my eyes across the room to where Kade stands with his parents and another couple that he introduced as his godparents, Maurice and Danielle Hollis. The tension that had invaded him in the town car had abated. But he still seemed guarded, not the open, smiling man I'd become accustomed to over the last few months since Lennon reunited with King.

As if he feels my regard on him, he glances up, and our gazes snag, hold. A coil of warmth unfurls low in my belly, and inconvenient need spills through me. Will there ever come a time when I look at this man and *not* grow hot and achy? Blinking, I shift my attention back to Tracey. Pretend. This is all pretend. He specifically chose me for this charade because I wouldn't confuse pretense with reality. There was nothing fake about the lust he stirred in me, but I can't allow myself to confuse attraction with what we're doing here.

"See? That right there." Tracey grins, looking in the direction of her brother and parents, then back at me. "I swear, I just got pregnant watching the two of you."

I loose a startled laugh, and her smile widens. "I have no idea how to respond to that."

"No need." She lifts her glass of wine and sips.

"It's amazing to see my baby brother in love and happy. And even more amazing that he's here. I've missed him so much. That's why, in my book, you're a miracle worker. And it makes us best friends by default."

I have no idea how that logic works, but hey, she's happy. Or maybe it's the wine.

"From what Kade told me, your parents have flown out to see him. You, too?" I ask.

She nods. "Not as often as them. I'm an obstetrician and don't get a ton of time off. But when I could, I made it out to L.A. with my parents. Between you and me?" Her voice lowers to a whisper, and she leans closer. "I'm a huge Bloody Sunday fan. I love seeing them in concert. Sometimes it's still hard to believe the same little pain in the ass that drove us crazy playing in the basement is *the* Kade Gibson, world famous drummer."

"I bet you brag about him behind his back."

Rolling her eyes, she lifts her glass for another sip. "Maybe just a little. But that stays here. That head is big enough already."

"I heard that." Kade's chest presses against my back, his arm sliding around my waist. "I always knew you were a fan girl."

Tracey balls up her face. "I don't know what you *think* you heard. I was talking about Imagine Dragons."

"Bullshit."

As they go back and forth, I try not to whimper in delight and need. *Part of the pretense. Part of the pretense. He's holding you as part of the pretense.* And that dick at my back is just a pure physiological reaction. Men get hard at anything—ice cream, peaches, holes in walls. It doesn't mean anything.

Doesn't stop me from relaxing into him and pressing against that erection.

I'm in such deep trouble. Like, you-can-get-it-let-me-be-your-sneaky-link trouble.

"You're such a little shit." Tracey snorts, but her wide grin ruins the insult. "No wonder Mom—hey, Jeremy. I didn't hear you come in."

Kade stiffens behind me, and the arm banded around my stomach tightens to the point of being uncomfortable. But I don't try to squirm away from him or ask him to let me go. No, I slide my arm on top of his and tangle our fingers. Just from his reaction, I know who just spoke. And if I hadn't guessed, the strain that enters Tracey's smile relays it.

"Hey, Trace," a man who's Kade's clean-shaven replica with close cut dark blond hair greets Tracey with a kiss to the cheek.

He's just a couple of inches shy of Kade's height, but that still makes him a giant to me. Like Kade and Tracey, he shares the same light green eyes. He, too, is clothed in a suit, his a dark blue with subtle pin-stripes. He exudes confidence and the same casual air of affluence that his family and godparents do. But as he turns and faces Kade, the smile he had for his sister ebbs then disappears, leaving him stoic and unreadable. Or maybe it does to the rest of them. I don't know if anyone else picks up on it, but I sense the hint of nerves in the slight flex of his fingers, and in the way his eyes flicker to Kade then drift away before looking at him again.

Kade doesn't speak, and none of the stiffness in his big frame abates. The tension pulls so taut it's crackling like static.

"Hi, you must be Jeremy." I lean forward and extend my hand toward Kade's brother. Lean, because

Kade's holds me in place. "I'm Lena Graves. I'm so pleased to meet more of Kade's family."

Jeremy hesitates for a second then he grasps my hand, and I didn't think it was possible, but Kade goes even more rigid behind me.

"It's nice to meet you, Lena." Only when I draw my arm back does Kade relax. A little bit. Jeremy nods. "Kade. It's good to see you, too."

There's a long, seemingly endless pause, and I silently groan. Tracey glances back and forth between her brothers, and the sadness darkening her bright gaze is heartbreaking. I squeeze Kade's fingers, and after a moment, he squeezes mine back.

"Jeremy."

Though his voice is hard, flat, at least he spoke. And when Tracey briefly closes her eyes, her shoulders dropping, I want to turn around and hug Kade. Then give one to his sister.

I frown. "I have to tell you, the genes in this family are like Super Saiyan strong. I'm really trying to be a good sport about it but secretly, I'm hating."

Tracey laughs, and Jeremy's face softens a fraction, a flicker of a smile twitching his mouth. Kade's snort vibrates against my back, and he loosens his half embrace to slide a hand up my back and threads his fingers through my locs. He tilts my head back with a gentle tug and I obey the silent command and meet his gaze.

"What do you know about *Dragon Ball Z*?"

"Boy, please." I scoff, waving his question off with a flip of my hand. "Vegeta was my first crush."

He arches an eyebrow. "You do know he was the villain, right?"

"Uh, correction." I pop up a finger. "Anti-hero. Get it correct. And your point is...?"

A slow smile curves his lips, and a pit yawns wide in my stomach, and a river of emotion pours inside. Not lust. Well, not just lust. If it were just that, sparks of panic wouldn't trip down my spine. No, there's affection, warmth and even pride at winning that smile like it's a damn prize.

"I see we have a newcomer in our midst." A gorgeous woman with dark brown hair and eyes the color of a summer sky slinks close to Jeremy, slipping her arm between his and his torso.

An emerald sheath that would've been conservative if not for the immaculate fit and the deep plunge between her breasts clothes a tall, slender body. For a second, I feel like a child playing dress up next to her —but only for a second. Fuck that. I'm cute as hell. And if this is the infamous ex-girlfriend turned brother's wife, then I don't have shit to be ashamed of. She does, and that inside doesn't even come close to matching the outside.

"Hi." Plastering a wide smile on my face, I extend my hand to her as I had Jeremy moments earlier. "I'm Lena. And you are?" I ask, knowing perfectly well who she is, but sue me. I'm in the mood to be petty.

She manages to tear her stare from Kade and lowers it to me. Slowly, as if she'd rather do anything else but touch me, she gives me the limpest and quickest handshake since the creation of Emily Post etiquette.

"A pleasure," she murmurs. "I'm Mira Gibson."

Am I supposed to pretend that I didn't hear her emphasis on the last name?

Oh, girl. Is this what we're going to do?

Apparently, I fight not to roll my eyes when she shifts her attention back to Kade, and her smile turns sultry, her gaze hooded.

"Kade, it's been a long time. Years. It's so great to finally have you back home," she damn near purrs.

"Mira." Kade's greeting is just as clipped and cold as the one he gave his brother. And that tension returns to his body.

I hate that. Hate it for him. And suddenly, I'm glad I came with him. Buffer, fake girlfriend, whatever—he needs me. That couldn't be more crystal clear in this moment. And dammit, I'm about to earn my fucking tuition.

"Oh, *Mira*," I say, injecting a surprise in my voice that's as fraudulent as my relationship with Kade. I tip my head back, meeting Kade's narrowed gaze. "This is your sister-in-law?" Suspicion flickers in his eyes, but he nods, the movement hesitant. "I've heard so much about you, Mira." I turn back to her, my smile still in place. Ignoring the panic that flickers across Tracey's expression and the slight hardening of both Mira and Jeremy's faces, I shake my head. "Wow. You're gorgeous. What? Do all the pretty people travel in herds?"

Tracey's relief is damn near perceptible, and it echoes in her laughter. Behind me, Kade softly snorts.

"I *really* like you, Lena," Tracey says.

I shift to the side and wrap an arm around Kade's back, sliding him a wry glance.

"See, baby?" I wave a hand back and forth between Kade and Tracey. "That's how you use your words. Do you want to know how he told me we were together? Told me, mind you. Not ask."

"Oh yes, please," Tracey says, rubbing her hands together in glee.

"I went to one of their concerts, and when security checked my backstage pass, he said, 'Oh, you're the girlfriend.' The arena personnel literally knew before me."

As Tracey laughs, Kade shrugs. "What can I say? I'm a man of action."

Smirking, I reach up and rub my thumb over his bottom lip. "Yeah, you are."

Oh, God.

The heat that radiates from that gaze. Whether it's for our audience of three or just for me, I don't know. Don't care. I'm singed. And when he encircles my wrist and places a soft kiss to my palm, my pussy contracts so hard I'm in danger of passing out.

His mother announces that dinner's ready, and I forcibly rip my stare from his.

It's all an act. It's all an act. It's all an act, dammit.

If the mantra sounds a bit desperate, well, that's because I am.

If I don't get it together, I'm in danger of throwing my heart at this man along with my pussy.

And that would be an utter disaster. For me.

"Lena, I have to admit I'm so curious about the woman my prodigal son brought home," Charlene Gibson says, the smile wreathing her lovely face echoing in her voice. "Are you from Pike's End? That's the name of the town, isn't it?"

I lower my forkful of the best glazed salmon that has ever graced my taste buds to my plate. I might've composed a love sonnet to it after the first bite.

"Yes. Born and raised. It's a small town and comes with all the stereotypes you've ever heard about one as Kade can no doubt verify—y'know, everything shuts down by seven, everyone in everyone else's business." I laugh. "But it's very pretty, has a great sense of community, and it's home."

"We haven't been able to visit yet since Kade moved there, but we have to make it a priority now hearing you talk about it," Charlene says.

"There can't be many forms of entertainment. You must get bored quickly." Mira directs her statement toward me, but her blue gaze is firmly fixed on Kade. As if her own damn husband isn't seated right next to her.

I shrug. "Not really, but then I grew up there. It's all I know other than the occasional trips to Seattle. But like any place, it's what you make it. Now I can't speak for Mr. Rock Star here." I nudge his arm with mine. "After all the partying and debauchery of your past, it might be a little too quiet, huh?"

He smirks, resting his arm along the back of my chair.

"It has its appeal."

"Look at you being charming and sweet in front of your mother." I arch an eyebrow. "Just carry that energy back home."

Everyone at the table laughs except for Jeremy, Mira and Kade. Humor glints in his bright eyes and a smile tugs at his mouth. Jeremy stares at me then Kade, his expression thoughtful, considering. And Mira? Well, she's stone-faced like she just found a fly in her salmon.

Score one for Team Petty.

"Okay, Lena, you told us how you found out about being his girlfriend." Tracey leaning forward from the other side of Kade. "Now how did you two meet?"

I relay our cover story—minus my fun embellishments—Kade interjecting every so often with a dry comment. By the time I finish, the entire table is once again in laughter, except for, of course, Jeremy and

Mira. She doesn't try to hide her displeasure, her full mouth flattened in a red painted line.

"That's so cute," Mira says, and out the corner of my eye, I catch Charlene's frown before she smoothes her face. "And what is it that you do, Nena?"

"Lena."

"That's right. I'm so sorry."

Sure you are. Heffa.

"No problem, I know it's a hard one to remember." From the other side of Kade, I catch Tracey's cough that, if I'm not mistaken, sounds a bit like a laugh. Mira's eyes narrow but my smile is a permanent fixture on my face. "And I'm an administrative assistant at the local elementary school."

Mira tilts her head. "Oh, a secretary. How cute."

This time, Charlene's frown doesn't disappear as she glares at her daughter-in-law. But Mira's little slick comment bounces off me. Better people—and by "better" I mean, "worst" people—than her have taken jabs at me. Still... She gon' fuck around and find out with that "cute."

Next to me, Kade stiffens, then leans slightly forward, but I lay a hand on his thigh. I appreciate him being willing to defend me, but Mira is amateur hour. I grew up with a narcissist for a parent and dated one for two years. I got this.

Besides, Mira is doing all of this to grab his attention. Nah, bitch. As his fake girlfriend, all his fake attention is on me and our fake relationship. You can't have any.

"I think so," I reply to her, keeping my voice light. "Getting to wake up every morning and be able to go to a job that I love isn't just cute, it's a blessing. Assisting in keeping organized chaos under control as well having the pleasure of seeing children grow, learn and thrive while helping them and their parents is a joy. Not to say some of those children and parents can drive me to day drinking." I chuckle, and it's real. "What's the saying? When you're paid to do what you love it isn't work. Or something like that."

Quiet settles over the table and the room, and Charlene stares at me, wearing a soft smile. And maybe I'm projecting, but I think that's approval in her light green eyes. Kade, cradles the back of my neck, then sends shock and pleasure careening down my spine with a kiss to my temple.

"Well said, Lena," Mason, his father, says. "When you have a passion for your job, it helps make even the bad days worth it."

"Oh, most definitely." I laugh again. "But one thing I can say, it's never boring. Even when I have intercessory prayer for boredom. Just a little bit."

From across the table, Danielle, Kade's godmother, nods. "So true. Our son is a high school teacher. The stories he brings home." She gives an exaggerated shudder then chuckles.

"Oooh, Lena, you have to tell us a story. What's one of the craziest things that has happened at your school?" Tracey asks.

For the next ten minutes, Danielle and I swap tales, and the more laughter and chatter everyone at the table shares, the more sullen Mira's face becomes. I'm not fluent in mean girl, but I'm pretty sure she's calling me all kinds of bitches and hoes—with a hard "r." Why does that brighten my mood?

"Still, it's hard to believe you and Kade have much in common. It must be a fantasy come true for you. The common girl getting the attention of the superstar." She chuckles, and the phony sound scrapes over my nerves like a blade saw. "The secretary and the rock star. Sounds like a fairy tale."

Like a record scratch, the room plunges into a deafening and awkward silence. Rage blasts from Kade, a low rumble rolls in his chest, warning of an imminent explosion.

But before he can let all that fury fly, Jeremy snaps, "Mira, enough. You're embarrassing yourself."

Well...damn.

I can't tell who's more stunned, Mira or everyone else at the table. One glance at the cold, forbidding mask on Jeremy's face, and she wisely shuts up, though her mouth curves down in a pout.

"Now that that's done," Mason says, throwing his daughter-in-law a dark look, "Kade, how's King? I told him I'm claiming the role of honorary grandfather for Gunner. Especially since none of my children seem in a hurry to give me grandchildren of my own."

"Dad," Tracey whines. "Really?"

The dinner conversation is harmless and teasing, but I know one thing that I didn't when I arrived at Kade's parents' home. Actually, two things.

One, Jeremy and Mira's marriage isn't a happy one.

And two, Mira's pursuit of Kade isn't limited to DMs.

Is it too late to renegotiate terms with Kade for hazard pay and legal fees?

Just asking.

4

Kade

From all the Sunday schools and church services my parents forced me to attend until I was sixteen, I know hell is a horrible place full of fire and torture.

Still, I bet if the devil himself was at that dinner table tonight, he would've hightailed his ass back to the comforts of his fire and brimstone pit.

Christ.

I rub a palm across the back of my neck, lifting the tumbler of whiskey to my mouth with the other hand. As soon as Lena and I arrived at the penthouse I keep here, I got rid of that suffocating suit jacket and kicked off my shoes and socks. And because I still felt like I was strangling, I jerked open the first three buttons of my shirt and rolled the sleeves up. All of that helped, but the shot of alcohol... Just thinking about the evening at my parents' home has my throat slowly tightening again.

For the last week, nerves have become a perma-nent squatter in my chest and gut. And tonight, walking into the home embedded with so many memories? I'd been more anxious than the first time I walked out onto a stage to perform in front of an audience. At least then I'd had the drum kit to hide behind, to lose myself in.

But in that fishbowl tonight, all eyes had been on me, the scrutiny like a whole colony of ants marching across my skin. It'd seemed like everyone watched to see my reaction to being home after so long. I silently snort. Probably to see if I'd sulk. Flip a fucking table. The sensation had only worsened when Jeremy and Mira arrived. Thank God for Lena and the bubbly distraction and deflection she caused, or else I probably would have been out of there much earlier, unable to stand being the focus of such expectations, attention and...hope.

That hope was the worst of the three. The burden of it—the weight of my parents' and sister's desire for all of us to be one happy, whole family again—sat on my chest like a five-hundred-pound barbell.

Shit.

I raise my glass for another sip, hoping it'll drown out the bitterness sitting at the back of my throat. It hasn't so far, but I'm no quitter.

"Oh, my God, Kade. This place is *insane*. I didn't get a chance to tell you that earlier." Lena, barefoot and still in that cute as fuck dress, appears beside me, a glass of wine in her hand.

She'd worn contacts to the dinner, but at some point, since arriving, she'd switched them out for her blue-rimmed, schoolteacher glasses. I don't know which version I like best; they're both beautiful and way too fascinating and alluring.

"Thanks."

I turn halfway around, surveying the penthouse as if seeing it through her eyes. Glass walls in every room offer a stunning, panoramic view of Boston Harbor, Boston Common and the Charles River. With the open floor plan, the living and dining rooms, kitchen, three bedrooms and four bathrooms all flow into each other. Hardwood floors throughout, a fireplace in every room except the kitchen, and cathedral ceilings make the already enormous space appear even more vast. The selling points for me had been the view and the loggia terrace off the living room.

As beautiful as the penthouse is, it's just a place to crash when I'm in the city. Nothing more, nothing less. It contains all the amenities and luxury items like state of the art appliances in the kitchen and expensive art on the walls, but my place in Pike's End has more...character. Not to mention, I feel more at home there. I didn't realize that until this moment.

"I can tell you had nothing to do with the decorating, though."

I glance down at her, feeling myself smile at her scrunched up face.

"Yeah? How do you know that?"

"Don't get me wrong; this place is gorgeous. And I'm going to enjoy the hell out of it for the next four days. But it's not...you. It's too simple, sleek. Too stylish and put-together. Part of me is afraid to smudge all this glass or dirty the couch with my ass."

I shake my head, but something tight and not necessarily welcome unfurls in my chest. As she's pointed out to me several times before, we barely know each other. Before that night in the club, we hadn't shared a real conversation. Yet... Yet she's right. I'm not entirely comfortable with the slick design. But I hadn't cared enough to give the interior decorator any input. I gave her a blank check and told her to do what she wanted.

And she'd made it more of a showpiece than a home. But there's no way Lena could know that.

She does, though.

And that's more disturbing than it should be.

"You're right, I didn't decorate this place. But I'm not here often enough for it to bother me," I admit.

"So you've been back to Boston but just not home?"

I nod. "We've come here a few times. But this place has been more of an investment property than anything."

She huffs out a laugh. "You know what my investment property is? My car and the water jug of pennies in the corner of my bedroom."

A crack of laughter erupts from me, surprising me since just moments ago, the last thing I believed myself capable of was laughing. But I don't know why I'm so astonished. This has been her all night. De-escalating the tension. Calming me. Soothing out my jagged edges.

I recoil, both mentally and physically. But she doesn't notice since she turns and places her glass of wine on the window ledge near the floor. When she straightens again, I've regained some semblance of control. And common sense. What do I, a six-foot-five man look like retreating from a woman nearly a foot shorter than me?

"C'mere." I can't move, but she makes it easy on me and shifts across the small space between us. Before I can guess her intention, she buries her fingers in my beard, tugging. "So how was it?"

"How was what?" I frown. "What're you doing?"

"Getting the real you back." She combs her fingers through my beard again, hiking up her chin. "How was it seeing your ex and brother again?"

"Fine."

Her fingers stop moving and she glares up at me. "Don't bullshit me. It's just us." She sections off my beard and starts braiding. "Now the truth."

She's. Braiding. My. Beard.

Now I know what she meant by getting the real me back. I briefly close my eyes, the pinch in my chest tighter, more acute. Yeah, I'd taken out my braids, put on a suit for the dinner tonight. The more conservative style had been my way of distancing myself from the shit that awaited me on the other side of that front door. But she'd seen right through that. She saw me.

That frisson of unease crackles through me again, but her hands feel so good on me...

Just for a little while. I'll let her have her way just for a little while.

"Kade?" She arches an eyebrow. "Talk."

I sigh, and unbidden my hands cup her hips, holding her close. Letting that vanilla and cream scent envelope me, tease me.

Soothe me.

"I was angry," I confess. "Still fucking angry. After four years you'd think it would go away, or at the very least turn to apathy. But no. Seeing him again, I wanted to tear him apart."

"Him?" Her fingers still. "What about her? Mira?"

"I thought I would be mad with her. Or even that I might have love for her still, and they would be mixed together. But surprisingly, I didn't feel anything. Not anger. Not love. Not bitterness. Well, hold up, I take that back. When she was trying to fuck with you, I was irritated as fuck. Good thing Jeremy got to her before I did." She didn't know how close she came to me going off on her. I didn't give a damn if her husband was right there. "But how you handled her tonight?" I huff out a chuckle. "That was a work of fucking art." And hot as hell.

She snickers, moving on to another braid.

"Why, thank you. I learned from the best. And by that, I mean Ben and my father. Not to mention his many girlfriends who tried to shade his daughter behind his back. Or in front of him." She shrugs but the corners of her mouth tightens. "I don't know you all that well, but I still can't see how you ended up with her. She must've put up an Oscar-worthy performance the entire time you were together."

"Believe me, I didn't see that side of her the first year in."

"How long were you in a relationship?"

"Two. And the last one I spent about ten months on the road touring. I would fly her out for some dates or manage to squeeze a day or two in here before having to head back out. I thought we were strong enough to last the separation. I never lied to her about how demanding my career was or how engagements, studio time, press junkets and meetings would claim a large part of it. And she said she was okay with it. But obviously that was a lie."

"Maybe she meant it in the beginning. Especially if in that first year you had more face time. Not that I'm excusing what she did; there is none for that. That's one thing I have to give Ben, even though he did it in the most cowardly way possible. Still, he didn't cheat and string me along. I don't understand why people aren't just honest when their feelings change instead of lying and hurting someone they claim to love."

Her words sink in.

"You might be right. Maybe she was honest at the start. And if I'm honest, I knew she was discontented. Not like she held her tongue when we talked on the phone or FaceTimed. But she didn't stop accepting my gifts. Or driving the car I got her. Or stop charging the Black Amex I gave her. You know what's fucked up?" My fingers press harder into her hips as I loose an abrupt laugh. "I caught her and my brother because of her. She'd been pressing me again about not spending any time together, so I decided to come home and surprise her. One of our concerts was canceled because of flooding in the arena, and we had two more days before our next stop. That was three days I could spend with her."

I stare over Lena's head, but I don't see the glittering Boston skyline. Once more, I'm in the house I bought for both of us in Back Bay. Climbing those steps to the second level, fucking roses and a necklace in my hands.

"I walked in on them in our bedroom. Not in the middle of the act but shortly after because she was in bed. And Jeremy walked out of the bathroom looking freshly showered and wearing only a towel. They stared at me, as speechless as I was. But I put the flowers and jewelry on the dresser then walked out of that house and never returned. Mira chased me, crying and begging me not to go but..." My jaw shifted as I ground my teeth. "The next day she called and said she and Jeremy had fallen in love and had secretly eloped over a month earlier. She meant to tell me the next time we talked. And in the meantime, I was paying her and Jeremy's way. I think *that* shit hurt just as much as walking in on them post-fucking. They'd played me, used me. Both of them. And I didn't believe she would've told me anytime soon. I still don't believe that."

She tugs on my beard, tipping my head down. Her hand brushes her fingertips over my jaw, and part of me wants to glance away from that too intense, too perceptive stare. But maybe because of tonight, a bigger part of me craves her touch more than I need to protect myself. So I let myself in indulge in the butterfly caress.

"What they did doesn't reflect on you, you know that, right? They took advantage of your heart and generosity, not just your absence. And that bullshit excuse about it being your fault because you weren't with her? That's just what it is—a bullshit excuse. She knew who you were, what you did for a living. She willingly signed up to not just be a part of your life but your lifestyle. And calling foul later doesn't justify her or your brother's actions. Especially when she's still benefiting from the relationship. Both of them should've come to you like grown ass adults, explained to you her change of heart and told you the truth. That's. On. Them."

I soak in her words like cracked earth absorbing the first drop of rain. And as she slides her hand down to cup the side of my neck, I lower my head and press a kiss to the crook of hers. I catch her soft gasp, and it goes straight to my cock. She made the sister to that sound when I first pushed inside of her on that office couch. And like then, it only makes me want to push harder, demand more from her. But unlike then, I back off; I promised her I wouldn't expect sex from her, and as difficult as it is, I'll keep that vow. Until the time she decides to release me from it.

"Thank you," I murmur.

She clears her throat and dips her gaze to my mouth before lowering it further to my beard. Shaking her head, she resumes braiding my beard.

"Of course. It's why you have me here. I'm holding up my end of the bargain."

"Of course."

Several moments of silence pass between us, and I can practically taste the tension between us. It's potent, like the whiskey I had earlier. And it's accomplishing what the alcohol couldn't—getting me drunk off my ass.

"Let me ask you something," I say as she finishes up and shifts backward. I rub my palm down her handiwork, not needing a mirror to determine she styled my facial hair in the exact fashion I've been wearing it lately. Three braids nestled within the beard. That shouldn't send a jolt of warmth through me. "Hearing how you talked about your job tonight, it's clear you really enjoy it and love what you do. So why are you returning to school so you can leave it?"

She bends down and picks up her wine glass. Taking a sip, she keeps her gaze averted, staring out the window.

"If I have the opportunity to return and earn a master's, then why wouldn't I? More education is never a bad thing."

She's deflecting. I can't say how I know, but there's definitely more there that she's not telling me.

"It's been a long day," she says, turning and surveying the penthouse. "I put my stuff in the nearest room, so I'm hoping it's okay to claim that bedroom? Unless it's a shower, I don't feel like doing anything else, especially moving my luggage."

"Your choice. The room you're in or another one. There are four to choose from...including mine."

The offer slips out of me without my conscious decision. I had no intentions of inviting her to share my space or my bed. But I don't rescind the invitation either. Her eyes slightly widen, and the glasses don't hide the flash of heat in the dark depths. My breath catches at that sign of arousal, and I go still, waiting... hoping... Even knowing it would be a terrible idea. We have boundaries and we shouldn't cross over them. But as her tongue swipes over her bottom lip, I don't give a fuck. I want her body pressed up against mine. I want her sweet and rich scent saturating my sheets. I want to slowly fill her up, feel those slick, tight walls resist me before welcoming me deep, so fucking deep in that pussy.

"I don't..." she breathes, shaking her head. "I don't think that's a good idea. I'll go ahead and take the guest room."

I nod, then against my better judgment, I pinch her chin between my thumb and finger, tipping her head back to look at me.

"I'm not offering sex unless that's what you want. If you find yourself getting lonely in that big bed or just want a body to lie up against, you know where to find me."

She doesn't reply but the rapid rise and fall of her chest betrays the effect of my words. Dipping her head in acknowledgment, she moves backward several steps, then turns toward the hall leading to the bedrooms.

Only once she's out of sight do I bend down and pick the forgotten tumbler back up, taking a sip.

It's going to be a long night.

5

Lena

I'm hookah-ing.

Nope, it's not a word, but it should be. Because this shit is good!

I close my lips around the hookah pipe, puff and the watermelon flavored smoke fills my mouth. I hold it for several seconds then blow it out with a low hum.

Through the vapor, I glance over the hookah lounge-slash-cigar bar. The laid back yet elegant atmosphere is amazing. Plush, circular, leather couches dot the vast space along with high tables and chairs. An elevated DJ booth sits behind a small dancing area, and a glossy, large mahogany bar occupies one side of the lounge. Pike's End doesn't have a hookah lounge, and they are missing out. I'm thoroughly enjoying the environment and the company.

Well, *most* of the company.

From my seat on one end of the couch, I eye Mira and Jeremy.

We spent all day together for a "family fun day" at Boston Common. *All of us*. While the games of kickball—his family might be wealthy as hell and a little bougie, but they can play some damn kickball—horseshoes, frisbee were fun, I still had to work very hard to ignore Mira and her flagrant attempts to catch Kade's attention. I almost felt a little bad for Jeremy—almost. I mean, he did some shady shit to get her. If you play fucked up games, you win fucked up prizes.

After the day of games, we cleaned up and went to Kade's parents' house for dinner. When Tracey suggested a night out in Allston at her favorite hookah lounge, I was game. But silly me honestly didn't expect Mira to horn in where she obviously wasn't wanted. So here we are, our uncomfortable group, pretending everything is copacetic.

And that I'm not about to strangle Mira with the hookah tubing.

I puff harder.

"We can leave anytime you want to," Kade leans down and whispers in my ear.

"Tempting." I blow out the smoke and scrunch my face. "But no. This is your time to hang out with your sister and get to know her man." I glance over at Tracey and Malcolm, the handsome man she introduced as her "friend." The way they're eye-fucking each other, I can see they're *really* friendly. "We're not going to let anything or *anyone* ruin that."

He nodded, pressing a kiss to the shaved side of my head before returning to his own hookah pipe. The touch of his mouth to me is innocent but my skin still tingles, turning up the heat that's always at a simmer when I'm near him. It doesn't take much.

I smile at him and when I shift my gaze away from him it clashes with Mira's. The other woman glances at Kade, lingers there then returns to me. A small smirk rides her mouth.

Huh. She's about to be on some bullshit.

"Lena, I can't believe this is your first time at a hookah lounge. They don't have one in your little town?"

I force a smile. "No, we don't."

"That's a shame. Kade, after living in Boston, L.A., Miami, you don't lose your mind in all the...quiet?"

Kade sucks on the pipe, eyes narrowed on her. After a long moment that bordered on uncomfortable, he blows smoke in her direction.

"No."

I trap a snicker inside at the flat one-word answer. Not that it deters Mira. I can't help but peek at Jeremy. His shuttered expression doesn't give any emotion away, but the space between them big enough to fit another person, relays a ton.

"I can't wait to visit Pike's End," Tracey says. "It sounds so pretty and peaceful. And just from the pictures you sent to us, Kade, I'm dying to see your house. It's absolutely lovely."

"You know you're welcome at any time, Trace. My door is always open."

"We should make a family trip of it," Mira interjects. "The past couple of days have reminded me of how much I miss just hanging together like we used to do. We used to have so much fun." She tilts her head, smiling. "Remember that time we all spent the Fourth of July weekend at Cape Cod? The food, parties, fireworks. Tracey, you had to leave early, but Kade and I spent a few extra days. I'd love to go back one day."

Wow. This woman has huge lady balls. First, bringing up a time when her and Kade were together in front of her husband and me, his fake girlfriend. And two, suggesting she'd like to "go back." And from the gleam in her eyes, I can tell it isn't the place she's talking about returning to but the position as Kade's significant other.

Again, I look at Jeremy and his face could've been carved from granite. Beside me Kade's leg starts to jump, and like in the town car, I lay a hand on his thigh. His aloof expression hasn't changed, but the energy pouring from him screams, "I'm about to go off."

"Really, Mira?" Tracey snaps.

"What?" The other woman strives for innocence, her blue eyes wide. Yeah, she's a D-list actress and no one's buying it. "That was a good memory and time for everyone. I meant no offense. We all have history, and surely Kade's...girlfriend knows that." She shifts her gaze to me. "Lena, you're not offended, are you?"

I part my lips to deliver my thoroughly sarcastic response but Kade beats me to it.

"If she's not, I am," he growls. "You're disrespectful as fuck. And if you're going to continue to talk shit, then be prepared for what you get back. Now if you don't want me to start *reminiscing*, then sit back, smoke or leave."

Damn.

I didn't think it was possible for Kade to grow more attractive but watching him shut Mira down on my behalf has me soaking my panties. Whew. I squirm on my seat, and he glances down at me, anger and something darker seethes in his eyes.

That was hot, I mouth to him.

His lips curve into a smile, and maybe it's the moment or the unexpected thrill of him defending me, but I reach up, grip his dark blond hair—now back in his customary braids—and tug his head down to mine. Heat flares in his light eyes seconds before I crush my mouth to his. I groan at the flavor of him—watermelon, a hint of his usual whiskey and sex. It hits me like a potent shot as I thrust my tongue into his mouth, sucking on his. I hold nothing back, opening my mouth wide to him as he meets me stroke for stroke, lick for lick. Only when an "All right, get a room. Or bathroom," penetrates the lust thick fog I'm wrapped in do I break the kiss. But Kade doesn't let me go without one last hard press of his lips to mine.

My breath is loud in my head, deafening. But it can't drown out the rhythmic pulse of need pulling my nipples tight beneath my shirt and bra. Or stifle the throbbing in my pussy. Thank God we're in a public place in front of his family. If not, I might have said fuck it, straddle him and ride his dick like my name was Annie Oakley.

He rubs his thumb over my damp bottom lip, and because I'm a glutton for punishment, I touch the tip of my tongue to the calloused pad.

"Excuse me. I need another drink." Mira pops up from the booth, and I turn in time to catch her striding quickly across the lounge toward the bar.

"Jeremy, you should probably go see about your wife. Make sure she's okay," Tracey says, picking up her glass from the table and eyeing her brother over the rim.

"She's fine. Or she will be." Jeremy returns to puffing on the hookah pipe.

I arch an eyebrow at Kade, and he gives a short shake of his head then leans back in the booth.

Okay then. Me and my wet panties are going to mind our own business.

～

ABOUT A HALF-HOUR LATER, I push out of the restroom. But instead of returning to the main area of the lounge, I make a left toward the screened-in porch I peeped after we first arrived at the bar. Turning the knob on the entrance, I step through into the shadowed area, the only illumination the hanging lamps at either end of the porch.

I suck in a breath of the crisp night air. It's May but the nights are still a bit cool. I cross my arms, considering returning inside for my jacket, but decide against it. Just a few minutes and I'll go back. Striding to the railing, I lean against the banister, tip my head back and close my eyes.

"Oh, sorry. I didn't know anyone was out here. I can leave."

I whip around to see Jeremy hovering in the porch's doorway. Part of me wanted to let him go. But this isn't my property; it's open to all patrons, including Kade's estranged brother.

"No, you're good." I wave at him. "I was just taking a little break before heading back inside. Please, come on out."

He hesitates, but a second later moves forward, closing the door behind him. For several minutes, we stand in silence, and surprisingly, it's not uncomfortable.

"Is this your first time in Boston?" he murmurs.

"Yes. It's always been on the top ten places I wanted to visit, so this is amazing."

"Has it lived up to bucket list status?"

I huff out a chuckle.

"From what I've seen so far, yes. It's a beautiful city."

"Good." He nods, slides his hands into the front pockets of his black slacks. Turning, he stares out at the back lot of the bar. "Kade looks happy. Looks happy with you," he says after a long pause. "I'm glad about that."

Not my business. Not my business.

"Are you?" I ask.

Yeah, well. Apparently, it is my business.

Jeremy glances at me, and a wry smile curves his mouth.

"I can see why you would question that. But yes, I am happy for him."

I stare at him for several moments, debating if I should just let it go. Kade didn't bring me with him for this. I'm only here to provide a buffer between him and Mira. So this time, I really am going to mind my business...

"Can I ask you a question?" I obviously don't even take my own advice. Sigh. Jeremy nods, and I shift, facing him fully. "Why did you do it?"

There's no need to expound on that question. We both know what I'm referring to.

Jeremy returns his attention to the lot beyond the porch screen. For a moment, I didn't think he was going to answer, but then his shoulders fell forward.

"Short-sightedness. Jealousy. Stupidity. Take your pick. Or choose all of them." He bows his head. "Kade and I used to be close. At one time, I even considered him my best friend. I looked up to him, admired him. And this was before the fame. He was just a good big brother. It's almost cliché, including him beating the ass of the prep school bully who picked on me when I was in the fifth grade. He protected me, included me in everything he did even though I was younger... I loved him."

"What went wrong?" I ask.

"The band happened. Fame happened. It didn't change him, though." He turned toward me, leaning a shoulder against the post. "Kade remained the same. At least toward me and the rest of the family. The world saw him as *the* Kade Gibson, drummer, songwriter and composer for Bloody Sunday. And, of course, his lifestyle change. He had more money, frequently traveled, people mobbed him, begged for autographs when we went out. So, yes, that changed, but he didn't. I did, though. I didn't even notice it at first. As I started to become Kade Gibson's little brother instead of Jeremy Gibson...the more I disappeared in the long, dark shadow he threw...the more my resentment grew. I was jealous of the attention from everyone— my parents, my sister, my friends, women. I became invisible and I blamed Kade for it. Instead of going to him like I would've in the past, I remained quiet."

"And the resentment built?"

Jeremy nods. "Yes. I'm not proud of it but there came a point where I was blinded by envy and anger. Then came Mira. She was beautiful, fun, witty—and alone most of the time. It started out innocently. While Kade was out on tour we would hang out with Tracey and other friends. But soon it became just us. Going to eat. Joining her shopping. Then dropping by her and Kade's house to check on her. I hate that excuse of, 'It just happened.' But that first time we crossed the line? It did just happen. But the time after that and the time after that? No, those were deliberate choices on our parts. And for the first time in years, I felt like I came in first place with someone. And it only made it sweeter somehow that the 'someone' was Kade's girlfriend. Finally, I'd beaten him at something."

I let that soak in. his words could easily be taken for bragging, but no. There's too much...disgust, regret in Jeremy's voice for it to be boasting.

"Why didn't you tell him? How long did you intend to keep it from him?"

"Pride. Fear. I didn't want to face his reaction. Even after we eloped, I think a small part of me was in denial about him discovering the truth. Until he did. And I lost my brother's, my parents' and sisters' respect, friends. It's been four years, and my relationship with Mom, Dad and Tracey still isn't where it once was. They've never said it, but they blame me for the fracturing of this family, for Kade not coming home."

I mean...

But I hold that back. I don't believe in kicking a man when he's down. Serving him a little truth, though? Oh I'm all for that.

"Jeremy, I'm not an exactly unbiased party, but I'm also on the outside looking in. And I understand how it feels to be in someone's shadow and invisible. It can be incredibly lonely and cold there." Main reason why I only called my father on holidays that involved turkey. "But Jeremy, you fucked up. Fucked up bad. You allowed petty jealousy, insecurity and your dick to damage your relationship with your only brother. And you need to own it. Not just with me out here, or even with yourself. You need to own it with Kade."

Jeremy blinks. Stares at me. It occurs to me that most people probably don't speak as bluntly to him. But hell, I don't have pretty words for this situation because there's nothing pretty about it.

"Look," I move closer to him and set a hand on his upper arm, "I just met you and I don't see a bad person. Just a man who made bad decisions. But because you violated your trust with Kade, it's your responsibility to make it right. This isn't something that's just going to blow over and Kade will forget about it. Honestly, I don't believe it's about Mira anymore—well, not so much. It's you he's angriest with because it's you he loves most." I squeeze his arm. "And he hasn't said it, but I think he misses you."

Jeremy's throat works as he swallows, and before he looks away from me, the moonlight bounces off a sheen in his eyes.

"Thank you." He clears his throat. "Thank you," he repeats. He softly chuckles. "I can see why my brother loves you."

Shock ripples through me, and my chin jerks toward my neck.

I can see why my brother loves you.

His comment strikes me directly in the chest, and it takes every bit of my control not to lift my hand and rub circles over my heart.

We're really nailing the performance, I silently congratulate myself. But the racing of my pulse is all too real. All too panicked.

"Am I interrupting something?"

Both Jeremy and I turn at the sound of Kade's voice. He stands in the doorway, backlit by the light from the hallway outside the bathrooms. A smile starts to curve my mouth, but his arctic gaze drops to the hand I still have on Jeremy's arm. Though it's innocent, a kernel of unease takes root in my belly as his face hardens.

"No," I say, moving towards him. "Your brother and I were just getting some fresh air and talking."

Kade moves out onto the porch, his attention solely focused on his brother. Once he reaches me, he slides an arm around my shoulders, pulling me to his side. Normally, I wouldn't mind being tucked up against him, inhaling that earthy, fresh and completely sexy scent. But right now? I'm just irritated.

"Your wife is looking for you," Kade says, voice

sharp steel. "It figures you're out here hitting on another woman of mine."

The fuck?

I tip my head back, glaring up at him. "Really?"

He glances at me then back at his brother, his expression still rigid.

"I deserve that," Jeremy murmurs. Dipping his
chin, he says to me, "Thank you, Lena."

He walks past us, exiting the porch. As soon as the
door closes, I whirl out from under his arm and jab
him in the chest.

"You're an asshole," I snap.

He crosses his arms, cocks his head to the side.

"I'm an asshole for stating the obvious?" He arches
an eyebrow. "He did it before, he'd do it again. I
wouldn't trust him with dick."

"Speaking of dicks..." I let that insult sink in, and
he scowls down at me. But before he can say anything
else that will have me dangerously close to wrapping
my hands around his thick neck, I pop up a hand,
palm out. "Nope. I don't want to hear it. If you had
taken five seconds to read the room, you would've noticed that we were just talking."

"You needed to touch him to talk?"

"Careful, Kade. There's no audience out here so
there's no need to sound like the jealous boyfriend we
both know you *are not*." His lips flatten into a grim
line, and I nod. "Unhuh. We were just talking, Kade,
and for your information, the subject was you. Jeremy
regrets what happened between the two of you and
wants to make it right."

Kade snorts.

"Okay, I'll give you that. It's not like he's given you
any reason to trust or believe him in the last four
years. But still," I step closer to him, scowling up at

him, "even if Jeremy was out here hitting on me—which he was *not*—you should have enough respect for me to know I wouldn't ever pull that shit. I'd never betray you."

His expression thaws, and he loosens his arms, and they fall to his sides.

"Lena," he murmurs.

"Nope, save it. I don't want to hear it at this moment. Maybe later, but not right now."

I stalk past him, and yank open the door, reenter the bar.

I hope he stays out on that porch for a minute.

He needs to be in time-out.

$$6$$

Kade

I fucked up.

Royally.

"Dammit." I stare at Lena's closed bedroom door, my fist raised but I didn't bring it down to make contact with the wood. Instead, after a few seconds, I lower my arm. And continue to stare at the door. Like a creeper.

I should pivot and go back to my room or the living room for a drink and watch some TV until I fall asleep. That had been the plan when we arrived home after leaving the hookah bar. Lena barely said ten words to me for the rest of the night, and my stubborn pride kept me from trying to draw her into a conversation or apologize.

Pride. Yeah, and a healthy dose of terror.

The dark, snarling and clawed thing that had rose inside of me at seeing Lena out on that shadowed porch with Jeremy had scared me. Not just the intensity of the emotion, but that it was there, period. In that moment, I wanted to drag my brother away from her and beat him like I hadn't when I walked in on him and Mira. The *need* to do that had been fiercer, hotter than four years ago. And that didn't make any damn sense since I'd been with Mira for two years and had known Lena for a handful of months. Hell, she'd been my fake girlfriend for two days. Yes, we'd had sex, but I've fucked plenty of women over the years.

None of those women nearly broke your dick and your brain.

I flexed my fingers, straightening them then curling them into tight fists.

No, Lena may be funny, witty, sexy as fuck, and contrary to what she believes, nobody's doormat, but she's still like any other woman.

Temporary.

Mira and Jeremy taught me well what happens when you blindly trust. When you open your heart to people who supposedly love you and care for your well-being.

They shatter you.

Unlike some, I don't need to fuck up over and over again before learning my lesson. One and done. And I'm so done.

Resolve hardens into a stone in my chest, lodging beneath my breastbone. Stepping back from the door, I turned and strode down the hallway, past my bedroom to the last room on the left. Pushing it open, I step inside and flick on the light. My drum kit comes into sight, and a calm immediately inches its way up from my stomach, spilling into my chest, throat. Closing the door behind me to the soundproofed practice room, I move toward the instrument that had saved me in so many ways.

This is what I need right now. To pound out my anger, frustrations and fears on the drums. To let it carry me to a space where nothing and no one can intrude. Not even sex gives me solace like they can.

Grabbing my sticks off their shelf, I walk to the five piece drum kit and get settled on the throne, my stool that has pretty much conformed to my ass. A sense of familiarity and welcome expand within me, and already my mind is clearing, and I haven't even settled my foot on the kick pedal.

Closing my eyes, I hear the rhythm in my head, my soul. I inhale, hold that breath for several seconds then exhale. On the tail of it, I set my drumsticks to the hi-hat, creating a shimmering sound before adding the kick drum, then the snare. Soon, I'm tearing into the intro of our latest hit, charging into the filler, and then finishing up with a crash of the cymbals. I don't stop there. I roll into another song from the new LP. And then another. And then one of our older songs.

I get lost. As always.

I don't know when I became aware that I had an audience. Sweat dripped from my face and slicked over my shoulders and arms by then, so I could've been playing anywhere from ten minutes to two hours. Usually, nothing invades that place I go to, but a tiny spark dances over my neck and down my spine. I open my eyes and find Lena leaning against the jamb of the open door.

Without faltering, I continue to play, but I can't rip my gaze away from her. Can't stop myself from taking a tour from the top of the bun she's gathered her locs into, down over her gorgeous, bare of makeup face, to the lush body covered in a tank and little matching shorts and to the slim feet and pink painted toes. I take a hot trip back up her frame, my eyes locking with hers.

Lust roars through me, and it's louder than the music filling the room. My gut tightens almost to the point of pain, and an electrical current races down my spine and farther to the soles of my feet. My cock thickens, stretches, and the ache there damn near steals my breath. I don't slow down, I don't slow down —I'm playing by muscle memory now, and her presence seems to propel me forward. Intensifies the driving beat.

This should terrify me.

No woman has ever effected my playing. Ever. It's my sacred space. But Lena... Fuck. Every crash of the cymbal, every thump of bass, every rhythm is for her. In some inane twist I can't begin to fathom, all of this is for her.

Maybe if lust didn't have its tenacious and relentless grip on me, I would throw her out, order her to never return. Be angry for this unwanted and frightening turn of events.

But I don't. I keep drumming until the song ends and the echo of it fades from the room. In moments, only the sounds of my harsh breathing punctuate the air. Standing, I set the sticks on the throne and come from behind the kit. I stalk forward—stalk because this feels primal and I'm starving.

Starving for her. And I want to tear into her with gulping, greedy bites.

I don't stop until I'm up in her space. She slowly straightens, pushing away from the doorway and tipping her head back to look at me. This close, the heat from her body brushes mine like a caress, and that rich, creamy scent is like a call of the wild.

"What're you doing here? The door was closed for a reason." I don't try to hide the growl or coarse note from my voice.

If it scares her, she doesn't show it. But that's Lena, I've come to realize. At her core, she's brave as hell, doesn't back down from anything or anyone.

"And yet I'm still standing here because you haven't kicked me out."

That mouth. *Fuck.*

I stretch an arm around her head, curling my fingers around the jamb. Leaning into her, I bow my head over hers, and I can practically taste a hint of the wine she must've drank since we arrived back home.

"You're standing here like I can't see those pretty nipples or that pussy. It's wet, isn't it, Lena?" I press closer until the beaded tips graze my chest. At some point during my impromptu concert, I dragged my T-shirt off. And I couldn't be more grateful right now. "You gonna let me find out, shorty? Let me get my fingers soaked in that sweet wet?" I lower my head farther, grazing her earlobe with my lips. I don't miss the hitch in her breath or the restless shift of her legs. Probably trying to ease the ache between her thighs. Nah, that's my job. "It only seems fair that I get to feel it since it's all for me. Since it's mine."

Her eyes close. "I don't think..." she breathes.

Lifting my head, I look down at her, taking in every beautiful detail of her face. The delicate arch of her brow. The graceful angle of her cheekbones. The stubborn line of her jaw. The prurient curve of her mouth.

"You don't think, what, shorty?" I ask, clutching the wooden jamb tighter.

She lifts her lids, and the desire gleaming in those hazel eyes are nearly my undoing. "I don't think this is a good idea." She shakes her head, but her hands gripping my waist belies her protest.

"Why? Or do I need to kneel down and ask your

pretty pussy for her opinion? What do you think she'll say?"

A breath shudders from between her parted lips, and her teeth momentarily sink into the full bottom curve.

"Kade." She lifts a hand and settles it over my mouth, and I'm dual parts amused and aroused. Amused, because she's trying to shut me up even if that red tint streaking across her cheeks tells me she enjoys my mouth and all the things I'm saying to her. And aroused because I want her to do it again. While she's riding me. "This isn't going to… end well. Last time," she lowers her hand, lashes fluttering as if her mind has returned to that night, "was an aberration for me. And you… Kade, you're the kind of man a woman loses herself in. And I've been there done that with—" I narrow my eyes, and she says, "Well, I've been there, done that. Knowing who you are, what you can do to me, it's not a good idea for me to do this again."

If she intended for her admission to douse the lust running through me with cold water, then she sorely miscalculated. Logically, it should give me pause, even turn me off. But hearing her admit how I affect her, hearing that wariness and need.

I'm a selfish bastard and I want it all.

"Do you trust me?" I ask, lowering a hand to pinch her chin.

"It isn't about that. It's myself I don't trust."

"Yeah, it is. I won't let you get lost." I tilt her head back farther. "Trust me to keep you, fuck you, give us both what we need."

She sighs, and the soft gust of air tickles my hand. She shakes her head, and my stomach bottoms out. Still, she's said no. I drop my hand from her face, step back. No matter how much I want to crawl inside of her, this is her decision, and I have to—

She launches herself against me, her nails scraping over my scalp then tunneling through my hair. A moan escapes her, and then I'm eating that moan. Swallowing it right off her tongue. Goddamn, she tastes so fucking good. Like every favorite dish and intoxicating shot of alcohol wrapped into one flavor. I'm instantly hooked...again.

My arms close around her, dragging her close. And I'm still not satisfied. I don't think this desire could be satiated even if I pulled her all the way inside of me. It's impossible but damn if I don't try. One of my hands slide under her locs, and the other fists the back of her thin top.

Without releasing her mouth, I hike her into my arms and carry her out of the practice room and down the hall to my bedroom. I shove the door open with my foot and stride into my room, not seeing the glass walls, the large fireplace, the blue and grey décor. I don't see anything but my bed. It's the only thing of importance right now except for the woman in my arms.

I toss Lena onto the mattress, and follow her down, covering her mouth with mine again. Not that she's content to be taken, claimed. Her fingers burrow through my hair, gripping the strands and holding me to her, licking inside my mouth and swirling her tongue around mine. I groan, slant my head, deepen the kiss. And each stroke, every lap, every kiss is like a hot, wet caress to my dick. She already has me hard and throbbing, desperate to drive and bury itself into that pussy that has haunted my dreams for weeks.

Giving her mouth one last hard kiss, I lean back and drag the bottom of her top up, not stopping until it's over her head, leaving her bare to my hungry gaze. Goddamn, she's as pretty as I remember.

"You haven't left me alone." She most likely doesn't know what I'm referring to, and that's good. My mouth is running, and my words are too revealing. But fuck if I can hold them in. I trace a dark nipple, nudge it with my fingertip. Her soft gasp is the loveliest of melodies. "So beautiful. *You're* beautiful."

I pinch the tip, lightly tweaking it and watching her face for any sign of discomfort. The first time we were together, she seemed to not mind my rough edges, but maybe that was lust and my own need. But she doesn't push me away. No, Lena arches into my touch, groaning as I pull and twist again.

Goddamn, this woman.

"Kade," she whispers, voice strained, a little high. "Please."

She doesn't need to say any more. I remember in vivid clarity how much she liked having her breasts sucked. And I give it to her, lowering my head and capturing a stiff tip, drawing it deep into my mouth. My groan and her sharp cry mingle, mate, and her nails scrape over my scalp. I switch to the neglected breast, tonguing the nipple while playing with the other damp tip. Lena arches and shakes beneath me, and I'm tempted to give her another orgasm with just breast manipulation—goddamn, that was so pretty and hot last time—but I want something else. Something I've dreamt about and didn't get to do when we desecrated that office couch.

Releasing her flesh with a pop, I pepper short, hard kisses down her abdomen. Her softly rounded stomach tenses, but I murmur...yeah, I don't know what I'm saying as I trail a path over her hip bone. I glance up her torso, meeting her pleasure-glazed eyes, and when she doesn't shake her head or tell me no, I hook my fingers in the band of her shorts and drag them and her panties down her thick, toned legs, dropping them somewhere over the bed.

"Shorty," I rasp, staring at all that beautiful, pink and brown, completely soaked flesh. "Why're you so wet? Why are you..." I don't finish that question as I palm her inner thighs, push them wide apart and suck her pussy into my mouth.

"*Oh, fuck, Kade.*"

Her scream echoes in the room, and her back bows deep, her fingers scrabbling at my shoulders, my hair. Her hips writhe, and I throw an arm over her, holding her steady. Because I'm nowhere near done with her. Shit, I've barely gotten started. And I'm so fucking hungry.

With a groan, I dive face first into her pussy again, devouring the thick juices covering her fat folds and swollen clit. I nibble and lick, stroke and lap, eating like a man bellied up to a buffet after a long, drought-filled absence. It's not neat or gentle. I'm wild between her thighs, gorging myself, and from the trembling of her thighs clasped around my head, she doesn't mind. No, Lena wants me wild and ravenous.

I swirl my tongue over her clit, circling the distended bundle of nerves and drawing it between my lips to suck and flick. Lena twists and undulates under my mouth and the graze of my teeth. And when I dip my head lower still, thrusting my tongue into her pussy, following it up with a hard, implacable thrust of two fingers, she shatters. Just like that, she comes for me, milking my fingers, pulling them deeper inside of her.

I stare down at her, as I climb off the bed, getting rid of my shorts, the only clothing I have on. With quick, impatient strides, I reach the bedside table, jerk open the drawer and remove a condom. The trembling slowly ebbs from her body, and she turns her head toward me, tracking my movements, her gaze locked on my fingers rolling the protection down my overly sensitive and painful erection.

I climb back on the bed, and with firm but gentle hands turn and position her so she's on her hands and knees in front of me. I shift closer behind her, sliding my hands up the insides of her thighs, and push them farther apart, leaving her pussy exposed and glistening to my gaze. God. How could she appear so vulnerable and rock strong at one time?

I want to shield her and break her.

Gripping her hips and tugging them back and higher, I slowly push forward, burying my cock inside her. A hiss escapes me; I'm unable to hold it in as her heated, wet and tight pussy clasps around me, welcoming me even as her muscles quiver in mild resistance. I pause, allowing her to become accustomed to my size and possession. I remember this, too. The work I had to put in just to have this pussy swallow me whole. The reward, though... *Goddamn.*

I take my time even though it costs me. I'm holding onto my control and orgasm by feather lights strings. When I'm finally buried deep, I exhale a pent-up breath, falling over her back, my hands bracketing hers. I lick the delicate curve of her shoulder, press a kiss just under her ear. Pleasure races up and down my spine at the exquisite sensation of her sex stretched and rippling around my cock. And though it's probably sacrilegious, I offer a prayer that I last long enough to get her off.

"I was jealous tonight," I hoarsely confess, pulling free of her pussy then surging forward and pushing deeper, higher inside her. She shakes beneath me, her ass pressing into my hips. "I hated you being alone with my brother. Hated you touching him. I don't care if it had been King or my father. I wanted your hands, your fucking eyes only on me. Only," I thrust again, harder, "me." I thrust again. Harder still.

Her breath catches—at my admission or the possessive strokes, I don't know. Don't give a fuck in this moment. Later, I'll regret exposing so much of myself to her, but now, it's right. It feels as right as the shrink wrap clasp of her pussy around my dick.

Leaning back, I grasp her shoulders, and fuck her with bruising back shots and dirty words of praise. She's the sexiest woman I've known, so uninhibited and free with her passion and her body. And as she throws her ass back, meeting every stroke, every grind, I'm lost in her. Lost in this lust that's starting to feel terrifyingly vital.

"C'mon, shorty," I urge, the slap of my hips against her ass punctuating the air, filling it with a lewd symphony. "Give it to me. Give me everything."

Yeah, I'm fucking greedy.

I don't want to leave anything on the table. I want her shattered and weak under me, knowing I did this to her. She's given this to me. I can convince myself that it's only me she will ever give it to.

With a growl, I press on her shoulders so her chest and face are shoved into the bed, and I fuck her with a fierceness that squeezes my chest and sends chaotic, electric pulses whipping through me. I'm so fucking close, but not without her.

Reaching around her waist, I thrust my hand between her thighs, circling and pinching her clit. She screams, the sound ricocheting off the walls, and her pussy clamps down on my dick, spasming around me, dragging me toward an orgasm I'm not certain I'll be able to come back from.

I pound into her, my hands gripping her hips again, driving through her orgasm and headlong into my own. Pleasure nails me in the back of the neck, the base of my spine and the soles of my feet. It all surges down my body to my cock, and I explode, a feral roar rolling out of me.

I slam into her, once twice, emptying into the condom. She sags to the mattress, and I follow her down, still connected and not wanting to separate myself, not just yet.

Lena told me we shouldn't do this, that it wasn't a good idea.

I should've listened. Fuck, I should've listened.

Kade

I accept the glass of golden champagne from the server with a nod of thanks. Usually, I'm not a wine drinker—even if it is champagne—but right now, I'm not picky. As long as it's plentiful and keeps on coming.

Sipping the alcohol, I survey the small ballroom and all of the guests packed into it.

Yeah, my parents actually have a ballroom in their home. And though this isn't the anniversary party—that's scheduled for tomorrow evening—they're tailgating before the big event with a "small" gathering. Family, friends and several business associates fill nearly every available foot of the room, laughing, drinking and eating hors d'oeuvres. And yet, this is just a fraction of the people who will show up at the hotel to celebrate Mom and Dad tomorrow night. They're loved, admired and respected, and even though I faked a relationship to get here, I should be happy for them, celebrating them right along with everyone else.

But that's the problem.

I can't focus on them when all of my attention is on that fake relationship. On my fake girlfriend. The woman I was balls deep in last night, and who I haven't been able to scrape free of my mind since. Neither have I been able to uproot the unease wedged beneath my sternum, steadily burrowing its way through my body.

As I've done the entire hour and a half we've been here, I search out Lena. It's like a reflex now, one I hate to admit to much less possess the compulsion. But that doesn't stop me from locating her across the ballroom, standing with my sister and Malcolm. Earlier today, I sent her off with Tracey on the pretense of finding the perfect dress for tomorrow, my treat. And while I wanted to give her something special, have her shine as bright as her beauty, it did serve another purpose. Space. Time apart. I needed both without her distracting presence to process what the fuck happened last night. And how whenever I thought about that cataclysmic mating that was everything dirty, hot, mind-blowing and too goddamn *special*, panic clawed at my throat. I felt like I was suffocating.

Like now.

As if sensing my regard on her, Lena looks in my direction, and even with the distance of the ballroom separating us, our gazes locked. And I easily read the wariness and confusion clouding those green and brown eyes. Lena being Lena, I'm sure she picked up on the distance I was putting between us. And a part of me wanted to comfort her, apologize and tell her I was sorry. But the other part... That bigger part is a coward and shrinks away from the need in me that won't be satisfied or extinguished.

Last night... That hadn't been sex; I've had sex before. Plenty of times. But the pressure that had shoved at my chest, the soul deep need that had gripped me transcended mere *sex*. It's ironic that I told her to trust me not to let her get lost in me. And it seemed like I should've made the same promise to me. I drowned in her last night, and even though I'm fighting and scrapping to drag myself to firm ground—to safe ground—I could feel myself losing to this *thing* that insisted on retaining its grip on me.

And I wanted no fucking part of it.

We had a bargain, an agreement. No feelings. No strings. Didn't matter if we fucked. We were two consenting adults, and the conditions still stand.

All I had to do was glance to the opposite side of the room to remind myself why those conditions needed to, must, remain in place.

Disappearing the rest of the champagne, I set it on one of the trays scattered throughout the room and headed toward the exit. If I'm going to get through this evening, I need something stronger. And I know where to find it.

Leaving the revelry of the party behind, I stalk toward the back of the house and my father's study. Grasping the knob, I push the door open and enter, flicking the light on while closing the door behind me. All of my attention zeroes in on the bar near the wide oak desk. Moments later, I close my eyes as the shot of Scotch I poured burns a path down my throat to mushroom in my stomach. I sigh, striding over to the bay window behind my father's chair and stare out of it into the darkness.

The door creaks open and I turn around, my heart thumping against my chest like a snare drum, excitement dripping through my veins even though I'd left the ballroom to put even more distance between me and Lena. But seeing as she followed me...

I frown, my grip on the tumbler tightening. Disappointment and anger douse the excitement as I watch Mira step farther into the room. Objectively, I can admit she's still a very beautiful woman, and the red, strapless dress clinging to her slim curves only emphasizes it. But my cock doesn't harden, my pulse doesn't race at the sight of her. I feel...nothing. Where once just the thought of her had nearly capsized me in fury, now I don't care enough to be angry or melancholy. It's just...nothing.

"What do you want, Mira?" I ask, taking another sip of the Scotch.

The corners of her mouth lift into a smile that I bet she believes is sultry, sexy. It's not. At least not to me. Did I say I felt nothing? That's not entirely correct. I'm tired and want to be done with this charade. Done with Mira. I'm ready to put her and Jeremy in the past and leave them there.

"I came to check on you, Kade. I noticed you left the party and wanted to make sure you're okay."

"I'm fine. You can go back." I turn around, giving her my back, dismissing her.

But this is Mira, and I miscalculated how fucking bold she could be. Slender arms wrap around me, and her body presses against my back.

"The fuck?" I snap, whipping around again and dislodging her hold on me. "The fuck are you doing, Mira?"

She smiles again, and I narrow my eyes on her, a disquiet crawling over my skin.

"Oh come on, Kade." She tilts her head. "It's just us now. Jeremey's not here, not the girlfriend," a subtle sneer twists her lips, "you brought with you. And if you don't think I can't see right through that ruse, then you've forgotten how close we were."

My heart kicks a hole against my ribs.

"Ruse?"

"Yes, ruse. You and I both know you only brought her here to try and convince me you're over me. And we also both know that's not true. You and I will never be through. We shared too much, loved too hard."

I loose a crack of sharp laughter.

"And I thought I was the only one who was hitting the hard liquor." I shake my head and take another sip. "I guess me not replying to your constant DMs wasn't enough of a hint that I didn't, and don't, have anything to say to you?"

"I know you're still angry with me, Kade," she murmurs, shifting closer. I almost retreat, but fuck that. I'm not running scared. There's only one woman who has the power to do that. "And I don't mind that. No, I welcome it. Because it only shows you still have feelings for me. That under all that anger still burns love."

"Really?" I laugh again. "I don't know where you read that shit but get a refund. Let me break it to you like this, Mira, but I don't hate you. And I damn sure don't love you. I feel nothing for you. Not one damn thing."

"That's not true." The smile evaporates from her face, and a stricken expression flashes across her face, those blue eyes I once loved to gaze into slightly widening. But it fades, too, and she frowns. "You don't have to lie. Not here when it's just the two of us. I realize I hurt you. I was just so lonely, and I made a stupid mistake—"

"This is old news. History, Mira. And we don't need to rehash it. I was there."

"Kade." She sets a hand on my chest, and I fight not to flinch from her touch. But my instinct is to slap her away. Instead, I gently circle her wrist and pluck her hand off me. She stares down at my fingers on her and glances back up at me when I let her go. "You love me; you know you do. That doesn't just disappear. I don't care who has come between us over the years. No one has touched me, made me feel like you, Kade. Now that you're back, I'm not letting you go again. I want it back. I want you back."

The weariness returns, and I pinch the bridge of my nose.

"Mira, you've convinced yourself that we had something we never did. Yes, I loved you—once. But I don't anymore. I haven't in a long time. I don't want to deliberately hurt you but what I felt for you..." I lift my hands, palms up, staring down at them before returning my gaze to her. "It wasn't the kind of love that survives what we went through. It's not the kind that withstands betrayal or apathy. Even if you hadn't fucked Jeremy, we still wouldn't, four years later, be a couple. We would've still ended up right here, you with someone else and me..."

With Lena.

I bite the words back, deny them even as they scream in my head.

"I refuse to believe that, Kade. I—"

"I don't care what you believe." I slice my hand through the air between us. "Go find Jeremy and make it work with him. If you put this much energy into your marri—"

Her lips cut me off.

Holy shit.

I freeze, shocked and caught off guard. But her moan and her tongue tracing the seam of my mouth, seeking entrance shatters my paralysis. Revulsion tears through me, and bile churns in my gut, making a break for my throat.

"Now it's me who's interrupting."

I close my eyes, cursing under my breath. Grasping Mira's upper arms, I set her away from me and turn toward the door, meeting Lena's cold and hard stare.

"Lena." I move around Mira and the desk, walking toward her. Needing to erase the hurt that flashes in her eyes before she shutters emotion. "This isn't what—"

Fuck.

She arches an eyebrow, as if daring me to finish that clichéd statement.

"Yeah, thought so. Don't bother." Lena shifts her attention to Mira, her lips curling in obvious distaste. Even though I'm so conflicted when it comes to her, and in pain at even inadvertently hurting her, that little sneer has heat pumping in my veins. "I've tried to be sympathetic and even patient with you. But pathetic bitches like you just won't let me be great."

"Bitch?" Mira scoffs. "It figures you would—"

Lena slams up a hand. "Yeah, I'm not trying to hear shit you have to say. But you should listen to me, because this is the last bit of grace I'm offering you. This one here," she points at me, "is mine. And I don't play about him. Put your hand, your eyes, even your fucking thoughts on him again, and I'm going to lose every bit of Christianity I have when I drag you from one end of this mansion to the other. You understand me?"

"Please. You can't tell me what to do." I don't have to look over my shoulder to see the unease on Mira's face. It's clear in her voice.

"I just did. Now get the hell out of here. Don't think I won't show out in this party and expose the real you to everyone. Including your husband."

Mira utters a sound of contempt, but she wisely leaves as Lena ordered her to, giving her a wide berth. As soon as the door closes behind her, I dismiss her from my mind, returning all focus to Lena.

"Shorty, that was not what it looked like. I know how clichéd I sound. I know that. But it just so happens to be true in this situation. *She* kissed *me*. I didn't invite it. Damn sure didn't want it..."

My voice trails off because I'm begging... and it's having no affect. Her face doesn't soften. And my chest cracks wide, opening a chasm that spreads emptiness through me.

"I believe you."

I frown, relief and hope coursing through me.

"Good?" Yeah, it emerges as a question because I'm not sure what's happening here. I don't understand the disquiet bubbling inside of me. "Why does it seem like you don't?"

"Because it doesn't matter."

"What? What do you mean? Of course, it matters. It changes everything if you know I'd never betray you like—"

"It doesn't matter because the damage is already done. Isn't it? It was done before we even left Washington and arrived here."

I spread my arms wide, shaking my head. "What're you talking about? I don't understand."

"You said you're over what Mira and Jeremy did, but it's not true. You might not love Mira anymore but her hold on you is still as tight as it was four years ago."

"Bullshit," I snap.

Her face, her voice displays no anger, no pain. Just a curious...calm.

No, not calm. Resignation. Like she's been beaten down and has accepted defeat.

It's wrong. Especially when she just unleashed all that fire and heat on Mira. This version of her is just... wrong.

"Bullshit," she repeats, a faint smile drifting over her mouth, and it, too, isn't right. "Why have you pulled away from me? Distanced yourself from me?"

I jerk my chin back as if the question slapped me in the jaw. Yes, I knew she detected something was off, but these questions hit too close, too hard. They're ones I don't want to answer. Don't have the courage to answer.

"You don't need to answer," she says, as if reading my mind. "You're either going to lie to try and avoid hurting me or give me the truth and it'll still accomplish the same thing. There's only temporary comfort in ignoring what's so plainly in my face. If this was even four days ago, I would run from it. But as implausible as it is, I've changed. You've had a hand in bringing it about."

She crosses her arms over her chest, and for the first time a devastating vulnerability seeps through, and for a moment, I'm staring into the heart of her. A heart that is bleeding. And for some reason, I think I've had a hand in that, too.

And I hate myself for it.

"You know," she whispers, staring into my eyes, peering way too deep, seeing way too much. "Yeah, you do." She nods.

I want to refute her, object and tell her I don't know a damn thing. But...I can't. She's right. I know what I saw in her eyes last night, what I felt in the welcome of her body.

Lena is in love with me.

And that knowledge has had me running scared all day. Has had me ducking and dodging her, the truth.

"You're not going to say it. I will," she murmurs. "I've fallen in love with you. I've broken our pact and didn't keep my promise. But you didn't either. You let me drown in you, get lost in you. I warned you not to let it happen, and you told me you wouldn't."

"I'm sorry, Lena."

"Me, too." She inhales a loud breath and lowers a breath, her arms dropping to her sides. She takes a step back and away from me. And I feel that step like a punch to the chest, driving the air from my lungs. "Because I can love you with my whole heart and soul but it can't make you want me back. It can't make you fight the grip the past has on you. It can't make you want to let it go and let me in. You're so terrified of being betrayed and let down again that you won't take a chance on what stands right in front of you—*who* stands in front of you."

"Terrified?" I latch onto that one word so I can avoid everything else she's said. Each word strikes me like small but powerful fists. "And you aren't? You're as scared as me. Don't forget I was there when you faced down your ex. I know the scars he left on you. You're telling me you want to go through that again?"

"Now you're just deflecting, putting up paper tigers just to tear them down. But I'll play along." She smiles, and it's the barest curve of her lips. "No, I wouldn't want to go through that again. But you wouldn't lie to me, denigrate me, abandon me. Even now, you're not doing it. You're abandoning yourself, your happiness. Because here I am." This time she spreads her arms. "And you're choosing to walk away from it. From us. But even if I didn't know with every piece of my soul that I would be safe with you, I'd still risk it. Because you're worth it."

My lips part but no sound or word emerges. But even if I could speak, nothing would prevent her from turning and exiting this room. I can't give her what she wants. Love. Trust. A whole man. But that knowledge doesn't ease the ache in my heart that threatens to burst. It's like I'm hovering on the verge of a coronary. I lift my hand to my chest, clutch my shirt directly over my heart.

But Lena doesn't see it. She's turned away and is walking toward the door. And coward that I am, I don't stop her. I *won't* stop her.

"I guess you're right, though." She stops with her hand on the edge of the door but doesn't turn around to look at me. "I did learn from Ben. A valuable lesson. Never again make someone else my number one when I'm not ever their number two."

She walks out of the study.

Leaving me alone...like I wanted.

Kade

This is déjà vu.

I'm back at a party. Drinking champagne again.

Alone. Again.

Only this time, instead of my parents' home, I stand in Boston Park Plaza's grand ballroom. The glittering chandelier and ornate arches over gilded balconies add an elegant opulence to the vast room.

And in the center of this ballroom, my parents are center stage on the dance floor.

I smile, a little in awe of them. Their attention isn't on their hundreds of guests but solely on each other. The way they gaze at each other, smile at each other, hold onto each other even as they move about the floor in a waltz is a thing of beauty.

An ache blooms in my chest, and I rub my knuckles over it. I love Mom and Dad; their loving relationship has always been a mainstay in my life, a source of stability in a chaotic and ever-changing world. If I could count on anything in this life, it was their steadfast and enduring love for one another. It's an awe-inspiring thing.

And, in all these years, the sight of it, being in the presence of it has never hurt me.

Shamed me.

Indicted me.

I almost want to turn away from them. But I don't —I won't. Because this is their night, and the adoration they share for each other should be celebrated.

They're fucking unicorns.

"And to think, I used to be embarrassed by all their PDA," Jeremy murmurs.

I stiffen, but I don't shift my attention away from my parents to look at my brother. I'm waiting for the usual unfurling of anger and pain in my chest—it's become a mainstay when I even think about him, especially since I've been in his company these past few days.

But it doesn't come.

Maybe I'm just tired.

Maybe Lena leaving this morning has taken every emotion I can summon. Everything I could possibly feel is wrapped up in her, and I don't have room left for anything else.

I take a sip of my champagne, watching as Dad dips Mom, and her laughter rises above all the chatter and applause.

"Yeah," I belatedly agree with Jeremy. "Now we envy them, want what they have."

"Yes," he agrees.

Now I glance over at him, taking in the perfectly styled hair, the Tom Ford tuxedo and black, shining shoes. We'd match if I'd bothered with a bow tie or cummerbund.

"I noticed your wife didn't make it," I say, not bothering to keep the contempt from my voice. I still haven't forgotten that shit she pulled last night.

"No." Jeremy looks away from Mom and Dad and meets my gaze. "I told her to stay home, that she's not welcome here tonight."

Surprise wings through me.

"Seriously? Why?"

"You really have to ask that?" Jeremy huffs out a chuckle that holds no humor. "I know what she did last night. I overheard the last of your...conversation with her. As did Lena. But when she handed Mira's ass to her, I didn't see the point." A faint but genuine smile that's reflected in his eyes ghosts across his face. "But when we got home, I ended what should've never been started in the first place."

"You left her?" I turn fully toward him, studying his face, looking for... I don't know. Truth?

"Yes. I finally did something I haven't had the courage to do and told her I wanted a divorce."

"Why?"

"Why didn't I have the courage to do it?" He slips his hands in the pockets of his tuxedo pants and turns toward me so we're face-to-face. And without snide comments and anger simmering between us. It's been a long time. "I guess because I needed what I did to at least not be completely in vain. I destroyed our brotherhood, your trust in me, our friendship. I needed to have something at the end of it all to say it was worth all the pain I caused. But," he shakes his head, "it's never been worth it. Not even one day, one minute or second."

"Why are you telling me this? You want forgiveness?" There's no heat in my voice. I'm actually kind of...curious.

"No, I don't expect forgiveness. Especially since

I've never said, I'm sorry. I've never apologized for betraying you in the worst way one brother can do to another. Never told you that instead of being grateful for you for always being there for me, I let jealousy ruin us. I was willing to throw away our friendship and fracture our family over petty envy. So I hurt you like a child throwing a tantrum instead of acting like the man you helped me to be. How can I ask you for forgiveness when I haven't forgiven myself?"

I stare at him, for the first time in four years seeing glimpses of the brother I'd loved so hard—still loved. I'd never stopped even when I told myself I hated him. If only it had been that simple.

And that's the problem. Love opened you up, left you exposed and vulnerable to be hurt. But...

But it sometimes offered healing and grace. Mercy.

Every so often, it even offered an enduring life with the one who completes you. Like my parents.

Like...

I briefly close my eyes, my throat working as I forced myself to swallow past the sudden constriction.

Fuck.

I look back at my parents, and a yearning so painful, so deep yawns wide inside of me in a place I hadn't known existed until I watched Lena walk away from me. Only then, I didn't want to acknowledge it. I convinced myself she was doing what would've eventually happened anyway—what was meant to happen.

I can't do anything about should've, could'ves. But I can mend this. Or start to.

"I can't do anything about you forgiving yourself, but you have mine. Maybe," I pause, turning my thoughts in my head, "maybe you had it a while ago. I don't know. I let bitterness eat me up, too. But I'm tired of holding on to that. I'm ready to let it all go." I glance at him. "Are we going to be who and what we once were? Not now but maybe one day. I'm willing to try, build our trust and work to be that again."

Relief shimmers in Jeremy's eyes before he closes them, but his shoulders dip. When he opens them and looks at me, there is hesitation there but also hope. That echoes inside me.

"Thank you, Kade." His voice thickens. "I appreciate that."

He stretches his hand toward me, and for a long moment I stare down at it. When his starts to lower, I grasp it, squeeze.

Then pull him into a hug that I didn't know I needed from him, from my brother, until this instant.

His body goes rigid, but only for several moments. In the next second, he grabs me in a tight embrace. We stay there, arms around each other for, I don't know how long. But when we step back, we've gained an audience. Our parents have stopped mid-dance and the smiles on their faces are brighter than the lights in the chandeliers.

I'm used to having the attention of thousands on me, but my skin is tight and hot under the eyes of the people in this ballroom.

"Okay, okay. More dancing," my father calls out. He pulls my mother close and kisses her to the applause and laughter of all their guests.

"They're the aim, the goal," Jeremy says as Mom and Dad dominate the dance floor once again. "The prize. You have that, too." He arches an eyebrow. "I also noticed an absence. Lena?"

I don't answer, clenching my jaw, trapping the words inside. Mainly because I'm scared of what would come out if I didn't.

Jeremy nods as if I have spoken. "I'm not trying to

be an armchair psychologist, but I feel like Mira and I are responsible for this. You're allowing what we did to hold you back from being with her."

"That's not…"

I trail off before I can finish the lie. Jeremy cocks his head.

"What, true? I think it is. We may not have talked for four years but I still know you. Remember when Nolan Ward went behind your back and told Gracie Lord that you wanted her best friend, not her, just so he could date her? He was your friend—supposed to be—and what did you do. Shut both of them out, didn't speak to either of them again."

"I saw that bitch several years ago," I grumble. "Had the nerve to come to a concert and expected me to let him backstage. I told security I didn't know his ass."

Jeremy snickers. "See? And that was how many years ago? Fifteen? So I can just imagine how you've guarded yourself and blocked people out over what we did to you. Not many people have the honor of experiencing your heart. I think Lena has, though. And I bet that had you pushing her away."

"I…" I bow my head. "Yeah, I did."

"She loves you. And you love her. Anyone with eyes and half a working brain could see that. Why do you think Mira lost her fucking mind?" The corner of his mouth quirks even as his eyes darken at the mention of his soon-to-be ex-wife. "Kade, don't lose out on what they," he nodded his head toward the dance floor and our parents, "have because of what I did. I already have enough on my soul that I have to clean up. I don't want that on my conscience, too. You deserve more. You deserve love and happiness. All of it."

I stare at him, my mind whirling. With memories

of the past few days. With images of how Lena so self-lessly offered herself to me. Of her last words to me.

I'd still risk it. Because you're worth it.

You wouldn't lie to me, denigrate me, abandon me... You're abandoning yourself, your happiness. Because here I am.

Yes, I did. I let my happiness, my joy, walk away from me. I not only hurt Lena with my fear of letting go of the past, of being hurt again. I hurt myself, too. I was so ready to throw away *us* because I couldn't, *wouldn't* fight. I craved protecting my heart and pride more than a future, a possibility with her.

Holy shit, I'm an idiot. An asshole.

But not anymore. I wouldn't shrink away and hide anymore. Lena deserved more.

We deserved more.

"Tell Mom and Dad I love them, but I had to leave early?" I ask, already moving forward toward the ball-room entrance.

"I got you. Make sure you bring Lena back soon for a visit."

I throw my brother a grin over my shoulder.

"Count on it."

9

Lena

"Lennon, I'm only giving you an hour, max," I grumble at my best friend's back as she pulls open the door to Road's End, the local dive bar. "I had plans tonight."

She snorts, shaking her head. "What? To veg out in front of the TV rewatching *Wednesday* and tearing up a pint of salted caramel gelato?"

"Like I said, *plans*."

Laughing outright, Lennon pushes her way through a surprisingly thick crowd for a Tuesday night and makes her way to a table right in front of the postage stamp-sized dance floor. India Roberts, now Hunt, the vice-principal at the elementary school and her husband Asa already claim two chairs. Lennon sinks into the third and grabs my hand, dropping me into the fourth.

"Hey, Lena," India greets, her smile wide, and a hand on her small baby bump.

"Hi, India. Asa."

Asa returns my nod. He might be sitting in another chair but is as close to his wife as can be without sharing that seat. His arm encircles her shoulders, and she's nearly sitting on his lap.

People in love. Boo.

It's so overrated. And sickening.

Especially when my heart is so sore, pulling a shirt on hurts. Okay, so I'm being dramatic, but screw it. I'm entitled. My heart is broken.

I nearly swallowed my tongue to avoid asking Lennon where King was...if Kade was home from Boston. It required all of my willpower but I managed not to do it. I needed *some* of my pride.

All the good it did me.

I cried the entire way home from Boston to Washington. I know the flight attendants and other passengers in first class either thought I was having a breakdown or someone had died. They wouldn't have been too far off.

My hopes that Kade would let go of his past to see me as his future died. My dreams of a relationship with him did as well. Too bad love didn't work like that.

To make matters worse there were reminders of him everywhere. In my living room where he'd waited for me while I prepared to leave with him. In the school parking lot. Even in my checking account.

Monday afternoon, I almost fell out of my damn office chair when I checked my online banking account and saw my balance. Let's just say it had more zeroes than I've ever seen in my lifetime, and it's more than enough to return to school. Shit, I could pay for my education and a couple more people.

My first inclination had been to march down to the nearest branch and have them reverse it, do whatever they needed to do to get rid of it. But then I regained some common sense—and by common sense,

I mean Lennon. After arriving home Sunday afternoon, I'd called her and spilled everything. And I do mean *everything*.

She convinced me to leave the money in my account. Claimed I'd paid for it in spades and should use it to get my masters or to get out of my apartment and into a house. Or just let it sit there and collect interest *and* mold. She was right.

I might have lost Kade, but I didn't lose my future. Now, I had the chance to pursue a degree in library sciences. Or education. Or, shit, pottery making. I had *choices*, now. I had freedom to make moves that weren't hampered by finances or uncertainty.

And without concern over other people's opinions.

I'd railed at Kade about letting the past rule him, but I'd been the quintessential pot calling the kettle black. I was about to go back to school because of an asshole ex and a neglectful father.

No. Not anymore. If I returned, it would be my decision. If I didn't, it would still be my decision.

I guess I have Kade to thank for that revelation.

But it's all I'm thanking him for.

Yes, *fine*. I'm angry. And hurt. But I refuse to be broken. Broken hearted, maybe, but not broken.

"Lena?" Lennon covers my hand, squeezing it. "Are you okay?"

"Yes." I nod. "Why?"

"Because I've been calling your name and it looked like you'd spaced out. Are you sure you're okay? If you really want to leave—"

"No, I'm good. I promise." I give her a smile. "But I'm still only giving you an hour before I'm ghosting this place."

She grinned. "Bet."

"What're you two drinking?" Asa asks, rising from his chair. "I'm headed to the bar. It's on me."

"Whatever they have on tap," Lennon says.

"The biggest glass of Merlot they have. If it's not the size of my head, I don't want it," I tell him.

Snorting, he nods. "Yeah, got it." Looking down at his wife, he arches an eyebrow. "I already know what you're getting."

When he disappeared in the crowd, India sighed. "I'm going to be orange by the time I have this baby. He read somewhere that orange juice is good for pregnant women, and cartons of it are packed into our refrigerator." She props an elbow on the table, cradling her chin in her palm. "Oh, I remember the taste of tequila. How I miss you, tequila."

Laughing, I reach across the table and pat her arm. "It's okay. As your co-worker and friend, I will sacrifice and order tequila next to drink in your honor. It's basically the same as you having it."

India scrunches her face. "It isn't, but I appreciate the thought."

Just as I laughed again, the lights over the stage that sat on the other side of the dance floor flickered off and on. The noise in the bar dies down, and I glance at Lennon, frowning. Friday and Thursday nights were usually reserved for live performances. She shrugs, but the corners of her mouth quirk upward.

A loud wave of cheers rolls through the bar, and I turn back to the stage. My lips part, and my breath stutters in my chest at the sight of King stepping in front of the mic. King and the other three members of Bloody Sunday.

Unbidden, my gaze searches out Kade. And my heart constricts when I locate him sitting behind the drum kit. Given the lights on the stage and the lack of them over the rest of the bar, it shouldn't be possible that our eyes find each other. But they do. And he doesn't look away from me. I'm ensnared, and though my mind screams to look away, ignore him, I can't. My heart won't let me.

"Hey, everyone," King says into the mic. "Thanks for coming out tonight. And a huge, special thank you to the love of my life, Lennon, for arranging for us to take the stage here."

I jerk around and gape at Lennon, who grins wide at me.

Shit, I should've known something was up. Going to the bar in the beginning of the week? That wasn't my usual thing or hers. She set me up.

I should be mad. And I'm going to be. Right after the shock thaws and I'm fully functional again.

I return my gaze to Bloody Sunday, and my spine hits the back of my chair when Kade moves from behind the drums and walks the short space until he stands beside King. The lead singer glances at his friend, and a big smile slowly spreads across his face. King nods and steps aside, and Kade replaces him behind the mic.

"Hey," Kade says, and everyone—except me—yells and screams a greeting back at him. "So I'm not used to being front and center, and you aren't used to seeing me here. But this is a special occasion so bear with me." Once more he looks in my direction, and I'm trapped, unwilling to move or glance away. "A little while ago, I met a woman."

Whistles and catcalls echo in the air, and a small smile ghosts across his mouth.

"Yeah, well, you know how it is. Meet a woman. Fall for her. Fuck up. Then lose her. That's where I'm at right now. But I'm not satisfied with watching her walk away from me. She did that once, and this time I'm following her. I'm chasing her." He turned fully toward me. "And Lena Graves, I'm not letting you go."

A silence so deep had fallen over the place, I overheard the beep of someone locking their car outside in the parking lot. But when he said my name and declared his intention, the bar erupted in noise, damn near shaking the walls. Several people patted my shoulders and back, but I barely noticed any of that. All of my attention was focused on the beautiful man on the stage who not just announced his love for me but his refusal to walk away from me.

But he had—or rather, he'd allowed me to do the walking, and he hadn't stopped me. Had, indeed, let me go.

So what the hell was this?

A flash of anger took me by surprise, and I trembled with that quick blast of heat.

How. Fucking. Dare. He?

I'd sobbed until my head hurt. Called myself all kinds of fools for trusting him.

Hated myself for loving him.

And he thought he could ease all of that, make it all disappear with some words? I needed him and he'd abandoned me. I couldn't forget that. Couldn't forget how it made me feel.

Maybe he saw the emotion on my face because he stepped forward, moving closer to the edge of the stage.

"I know I hurt you, Lena. I broke my promise to you, abandoned you just like you accused me of doing. And you were absolutely right. You terrified me—shit, you still do. But it's different now. Instead of being afraid of being hurt, I'm afraid of not living this life with the joy, laughter, peace and love you've brought to it. That prospect scares me like nothing else ever has. I don't deserve another chance. But it's not stopping me from begging you for one."

"Damn," Lennon breathed from beside me. "You know I wanted to kick his ass for you, but girl. Say yes, or I will for you."

I couldn't utter anything.

I was afraid. Afraid of the hope that tried to creep its way up my chest and spread throughout my body. Afraid to let go of the security of the known to take a leap of faith on the unknown—Kade. Afraid to put myself out there again only to possibly be rejected.

Afraid to never touch him again, inhale his scent again. Never hear him say, I love you.

The possible cons of this situation far outweighed the pros.

But that wasn't faith.

Faith was stepping out into the deep believing you would be lifted up and set on a solid foundation, even if you couldn't see the ground beneath your feet. Faith was going against all perceived common sense to do something as crazy as trust in the precariousness and beauty of love.

I would choose love and the possibility of Kade any day rather than the bleak, lonely future without him.

Heart pounding against my ribs, I stand. For a moment, I'm not sure if my trembling legs will support me, but it doesn't matter. Before I can take two steps forward, Kade jumps off the stage and the crowd parts as he strides toward me, scooping me into his arms and crushing me against him.

I wrap my arms and legs around him, and the raucous applause of the bar's customers is dim background noise to the racing pulse echoing in my head.

"I love you." His bright green eyes roam my face before they meet mine. And he says again, I love you, Lena Gibson. So fucking much."

"I love you, too," I whisper.

His eyes close, and something that looks like pain spasms across his face. When he lifts his lashes, the emotion there steals what little breath I had left.

"You forgive me?"

If I hadn't, the uncertainty and vulnerability that saturates his question would've melted any lingering resentment. But I can honestly admit, he had my forgiveness the moment he stepped on that stage. Because he came for me. He was the first man in my life to come for me. There's no way I could hold anything against him.

"Yes." I trace his cheekbone, his bottom lip with my fingers. "Always."

He blows out a breath and buries his face in my neck. My arms tighten around him. And when he lifts his head and takes my mouth, I freely give him that, too, pouring all my love into it. He kisses me like a starving man, a desperate man, and he's just found the source of his every need.

"I've missed you, shorty," he breathes against my lips. "It's just been days, but I've missed you. I need you."

"Good thing I don't plan on going anywhere anytime soon. And by anytime soon, I mean never."

He laughs, and it's so free, so joyous, I join in.

"Uh, Kade. I don't mean to break up this moment, but we have a set to perform," King drawls into the mic.

"Fucking cockblocker," Kade mutters, but he grins,

planting another kiss on my mouth before lowering me to the floor. But he doesn't release me. He cups my cheek and presses his forehead to mine. "Stay?" he asks. "I selected every song in this set for you."

"Well, shit. How can I leave after that?" My inner fan girl is screaming and throwing her panties at him right now.

He grins, kisses me again. "Thank you for not giving up on me."

"Thank you for pursuing me and not letting me go."

"Never. You're stuck with me," he warns, and I raise on my toes and nip his bottom lip.

"There's no place I'd rather be."

ABOUT NAIMA SIMONE

USA Today Bestselling author Naima Simone's love of romance was first stirred by Johanna Lindsey, Sandra Brown and Nora Robert's many years ago. Well not that many. She is only eighteen...ish. Though her first attempt at a romance novel starring Ralph Tresvant from New Edition never saw the light of day, her love of romance, reading and writing has endured. Published since 2009, she spends her days—and nights—creating stories of unique men and women who experience the first bites of desire, the dizzying heights of passion, and the tender, healing heat of love.

She is wife to Superman, or his non-Kryptonian, less bullet proof equivalent, and mother to the most awesome kids ever. They all live in perfect, sometimes domestically-challenged bliss in the southern United States.

Visit Naima at www.naimasimone.com. Or connect with Naima through email (nsimonebooks@aol.com), through her website, through her newsletter or become a member of her fabulous Facebook Street Team.

ALSO BY NAIMA SIMONE

Secrets and Sins Series

Gabriel

Malachim

Raphael

Chayot

Guarding Her Body Series

Witness to Passion

Killer Curves

Bachelor Auction Series

Beauty and the Bachelor

The Millionaire Makeover

The Bachelor's Promise

A Millionaire at Midnight

Lick Series

Only for Your Touch

Only for You

Other Titles

Flirting with Sin